Living with Shadows

Joan Rowe

Matador
9 Priory Business Park,
Wistow Road, Kibworth Beauchamp,
Leicestershire. LE8 0RX
Tel: 0116 279 2299
Email: books@troubador.co.uk
Web: www.troubador.co.uk/matador
Twitter: @matadorbooks

ISBN 978 1788039 178

British Library Cataloguing in Publication Data.
A catalogue record for this book is available from the British Library.

Printed and bound by CPI Group (UK) Ltd, Croydon, CR0 4YY
Typeset in 11pt Aldine401 BT by Troubador Publishing Ltd, Leicester, UK

Matador is an imprint of Troubador Publishing Ltd

About the Author

Edinburgh pianist and writer Joan Rowe, a former history teacher and music lecturer, endured a chaotic childhood. Music and writing became her lifeline. An inherited WW1 navy diary inspired Duty (Matador 2014) and its sequel Living With Shadows. Joan has also written a memoir In Search of Home describing her 23 different homes.

FOR ALL WHO SERVED

Part One

May 13th 1915 – 01.15 approximately. HMS Goliath was anchored off Morto Bay in the Dardanelles Strait

Ship's writer Charles Richards had just crept up on deck for a crafty smoke. That was, until he spotted the Captain up on the bridge. Charles promptly buttoned up his jacket and hurriedly threw his cigarette over the side of the ship. The air was hot and heavy but still he was expected to be properly dressed, even then.

Close behind him was Arthur Cole, ship's carpenter. They had been friends since childhood. He had followed Charles up from the gun room, where some of the boy sailors were sleeping fully clothed, in spite of the heat.

'Poor kids, eh, Charles? They've no idea what's ahead.'

'No more than we do, Arthur.'

Both men, not actually enlisted sailors, peered out into the darkness and thick fog. They could only guess what was going on in the mind of the Captain. He appeared to be inspecting the ship's searchlights. He quickly indicated something to the officer of the watch.

'What do you think that's all about, Charles?'

'I don't know for sure, but it's my guess that he is lowering the angle of the searchlights.'

They both felt un-nerved, filled with apprehension at what dawn might bring. Arthur had made a swift estimation of their possible fate.

'If you ask me, we're just like sitting ducks.'

'We're anchored a good way out of the bay,' Charles said. 'We have *Cornwallis* and the other ships covering us.'

'How many troops are landing there tomorrow?

1

'Not sure, Arthur. We might have to rescue some. That's where the fighting will be.'

'Poor sods, eh, Charles?'

'Yes! Come on, we'd better not hang about here much longer.'

'What are you thinking about, Charles?'

'Right now I am thinking it's a rotten way to be spending my twenty-first birthday.'

'I expect they'll save you some cake, at home?'

Charles grinned at his friend.

'I've missed my birthday too, you know. Do you remember that there's only three months between us?'

Arthur had remembered that. In a manner of speaking they had almost grown up together.

Violet Cole, Arthur's grandmother had been the Richards family housekeeper. His grandfather, or Granda, as he was known, had been a master carpenter, a true genius with wood. He had made many fine things for Alfred Richards and his gallery in the big house at Kensington. Arthur had watched his Granda work for hours and hours. He had learned the trade and he loved it. He loved the feel of the raw wood and the feel of it when it had been fashioned and polished to perfection.

When they were children Arthur had been allowed to play with Charles during the school holidays. A great bond had grown between them. Arthur's elder brother, Jim, had run away from home to join the navy because he wanted to sail in the new dreadnought battleship. Arthur missed him. He hadn't ever wanted to join the navy, at least not then. All he wanted to do was to become a master carpenter like his Granda. He worked his way up from being an apprentice. He couldn't quite believe that now he was a ship's carpenter. He wasn't always making fine things. His work often meant repairing things. Still, it had been the most incredible stroke of luck that Arthur and Charles had found each other again, after four years apart. The two friends stopped reminiscing about home and their different childhoods. They heard some of the boys scrambling up the stairs to the deck.

'Cor, that's better,' said one, throwing his top off. 'I can breathe better now. It's boiling 'ot downstairs!'

Arthur corrected him.

'It's below decks, not downstairs, lad.'

The boy sheepishly apologised for his ignorance.

If the Captain were to see them they would all be in trouble. Charles Richards hurriedly found a place for the boys to hide, beneath a couple of loose tarpaulins.

'It's like an adventure,' said the boy's pal.

'Quiet, you lot, or you will be in big trouble. Don't move about, and whatever you do keep well away from the midships. Do you hear?'

'Why's that, sir?'

'Don't ask questions. Just do as you're told.'

Under his breath Charles uttered, 'Let's hope you don't find out.'

If they were destined to be hit by enemy torpedoes it was a pretty sure bet that the torpedoes would find the midships first.

For a while there in the darkness and under the tarpaulin the boys talked about home and what they would tell people when they got home again.

'Except for the grub,' complained one boy. 'I miss me Ma's cooking.'

'Mine'll be cross that we were given a rum ration.'

'But it's watered down, ain't it?'

Some of the boys drifted off to sleep again. A couple of them were humming popular ditties to pass the time. They couldn't sleep.

Charles Richards felt so uneasy that he couldn't contemplate sleep at all. Humming ditties was the last thing on his mind. He allowed his thoughts to wander to his own family. His mind was racing as he thought of his parents and his Aunt Alice. He tried desperately to say a prayer for them but he couldn't remember any appropriate words. Perhaps it was enough that he had thought of them and prayed that they had escaped the London bombs dropped by the zeppelins.

Charles wondered and hoped that the family had received the last letter that he had posted. He wondered whether Jim Cole had managed to give them his personal diary. He remembered his last meeting with Jim whilst they were on shore leave together. He had asked Jim if he would deliver the diary to his Aunt Alice.

'Just in case you get home, Jim, and I don't. Aunt Alice would know what to do with it.'

Jim said he would do his best.

Alfred Richards, Charles' father, would be astute and clever enough to read between the lines about all the navy stuff. He'd recorded the Rear Admiral's Inspection before they had set sail. He told of Winston's visit accompanied by Prince Louis of Battenberg. Perhaps he shouldn't have written about that. Frances, Charles' mother, would be just happy to have the diary. She would treasure it simply because it belonged to her son.

Alice would admire the beautiful handwriting. She knew that he always used the silver pen she had given to him before they left home.

Charles Richards shivered in spite of the heat and fog around him. He somehow feared that he would not be completing the ship's record that night, or perhaps any other night.

About an hour or so after midnight when *Goliath*, or 'Golly', as the men called their ship, was anchored off Morto Bay and under cover of darkness and thick fog, the worst happened. A Turkish torpedo boat, the Muavenet-i-Millye, manned by a German crew sneaked through the narrows and opened fire. After the first torpedo struck, *Goliath* keeled over and held steady for just a few seconds. Charles Richards yelled as loud as he possibly could.

'Jump, boys! Jump for your lives!'

He pulled the tarpaulin away from the boys who were sheltering there.

'Quick as you can, over the side. Go! Go! Jump!'

Charles had to push one boy who stood transfixed with fear and shock. Arthur Cole tore his own jacket off so that he might swim better. He knew he had to jump clear of the side.

'Charles! Charlie!' he yelled for his friend.

'Go, Arthur, Artie. I'm right behind you.'

The last thought trickling through Charles Richards' mind was just how strange that they both yelled out their childhood nicknames for each other at the same time.

Everything which wasn't secured was thrown across the decks, or over the side. Below decks there was a terrible noise of crashing furniture, fittings and crockery of every kind. Then there was the tremendous sound of screaming. All became muffled after the next two torpedoes struck within four minutes. *HMS Goliath*, 'Golly', was completely sunk. The good swimmers moved as fast as they could to get clear of the suction when the ship disappeared beneath the waves.

It was at least a thirty foot drop from the ship's side into the water. Those who didn't manage to jump clear scraped their bodies and faces down the side of the ship – some, so badly injured, that, mercifully for them, they managed to knock themselves unconscious before they hit the dark, murky water.

Goliath was gone. She had disappeared beneath the waves in just a few dreadful minutes. Some of the crew lay trapped aboard, imprisoned under the sea. Those who escaped the ship became part of the mass of floating bodies. Their cries became more and more muffled. Bodies were sinking in slow motion, competing with ship's debris and other bodies, as though vying for their own eternal space. Only the strongest swimmers survived.

The enemy torpedo boats had slipped away into the darkness and the narrows.

At about 1.30 a.m. messages were hurriedly sent from *HMS Cornwallis* and the other large ships to deploy as many smaller rescue boats and barges as they could. It was mayhem. The rescue crews were all shouting at once and were severely hampered in the darkness.

'We need more lights!'

'Keep steady, or we'll all drown!'

The rescuers had a thankless task. They did their best to pull men from the water and heave them over the side to relative safety.

It was almost impossible for them to know whether the men they were rescuing were alive or dead.

'Careful with this one. He's alive but barely conscious.'

'This chap's bleeding badly. Watch his arm!'

'Find this man a place near the back. Cover his face. He's badly burned and bleeding.'

That man's rescuers were both violently sick over the side.

The small boats soon filled to capacity with the living and the dead. They took as many as they could. The rescuers were anxious to get away and on to the big ships.

'Won't make any difference,' someone shouted. 'If there's another torpedo coming our way the only thing to do is pray!'

The hospital ships were anchored precariously further down the straits. The Hague Convention had decreed that hospital ships were not to be fired at, but nobody believed that the Germans or the Turks would stick to it.

The rescued sailors were transferred carefully from the smaller boats and barges. When the berths were filled up they had to be placed in a temporary space on the deck floor, wherever there was a space.

Observing the desperately chaotic scene, notebook and bible in his hands, was a newly-ordained young curate from England. Crispen Honeybourn should have been with the ground forces of Gallipoli. Somehow he had managed to get himself on the wrong transport. So, there he was, a young inexperienced navy chaplain, whether he liked it or not. It was certainly a far cry from his anticipated country parsonage in England, where he supposed he would minister to the gentle folk of his village.

Crispen Honeybourn was facing the most terrifying time of his life. He was frightened and overcome by the enormity of the task before him. As he ran aimlessly backwards and forwards between the lines of orderlies and the rescued men, he felt deeply embarrassed that he felt so wimpish, sick and faint at the dreadful sights before him. He stopped momentarily to push his horn-rimmed spectacles more securely on his face.

'Come on man, move out of the way!' bellowed Sister Mackintosh. 'We haven't got time to stand around. Perhaps you could help Nurse Flowers?'

Sister Mackintosh thrust a pile of blankets at him and he duly followed Nurse Flowers. Sister Mackintosh had not recognised the Chaplain's uniform and they had not been introduced. Nurse Flowers fortunately had her wits about her and took charge of the nervous young Chaplain.

'Don't worry about Sister Mackintosh, sir. Her bark is worse than her bite. She is a first-rate nursing sister and she has had more experience in nursing than any of us.'

Nurse Flowers began to weep through sheer exhaustion and frustration.

'There are so many,' she cried. 'We are having to lie the living next to the dying, Chaplain. It is very difficult to get between them to examine them and to dress their wounds. Some are so badly injured they just cannot be moved.'

The nurse looked pleadingly at the young desperately-worried Chaplain Honeybourn. Her frustrations and tears had, however, pulled him to his senses. He took on his full role, the role he was ordained to do. He forgot about his own nervousness and fear and took charge of the situation. He managed to find a couple of orderlies who seemed to be hands-free just then.

'Over here, men. Please, as soon as you can. We need to move out the men who have sadly died in transit. I have made a small chapel, a makeshift place for now. We must try to move them with care and dignity. Then the nurses can reach the injured more easily.'

The orderlies obeyed the Chaplain, who had suddenly assumed a sense of authority, not unlike that of Sister Mackintosh. As the Sister was out of earshot just then, he felt brave enough to take the initiative.

'That's it! Over here, men. Thank you. Nurse Flowers will tell you which ones can be moved next.'

The Chaplain had found an area suitable to lay the men out as decently as he could, though sheets were now in short supply. He said a short prayer over each dead sailor and felt deeply sad that he did not have their names. He improvised with his words as he did with the sheets and sacking which covered them.

Nurse Flowers and the Chaplain made their way back to the injured ward area to see what their next job would be. The two orderlies accompanied them, partly shielding them from Sister Mackintosh.

'Too late! Here she comes,' said Orderly One.

'She's like a galleon in full sail,' said the second man.

'Are you still here, Chaplain?'

Sister Mackintosh gently pushed him to one side, with the briefest of apologies for her earlier rudeness. He said that he quite understood what with all the confusion aboard. He tried to explain about the makeshift chapel. She thanked him for his efforts, if rather dismissively.

'Well, thank you, Chaplain Honeybourn. Very decent of you, though I wonder who will say prayers over us if we get the next torpedo?'

'Surely, The Hague Convention. They can't torpedo a hospital ship. Can they, Sister?'

'I wouldn't bet on it,' joined in the orderlies.

'Some of these men are very ill and badly injured. Many of them will not survive the night. We just have to get on and do the job as best we can,' Sister Mackintosh told them.

'All the more reason for me to sit beside them and try to comfort them, if I can.'

Sister Mackintosh huffed and puffed and hurried away. The orderlies found a quiet corner to hide away until they were needed. They doubted that they would get any sleep, but they might as well have a few minutes' rest, until called.

Nurse Flowers was exhausted too. She and the Chaplain both trembled as they knelt down beside a boy sailor. He hardly looked old enough to be there. The Nurse took his hand. He could only half open his badly-bruised eyes. He gave them a sort of smile.

'He is one of the *Goliath* boys. Sister Mackintosh told me that he hadn't managed to jump clear of the ship's side. He had a terrible bump to his head.'

'I've escaped, haven't I?' he mumbled through his cut lips.

'Yes, you did,' the nurse smiled and nodded.

The boy closed his eyes and slept again. Chaplain Honeybourn said a prayer over him and then stood to meet the orderlies who would be needed again. As he turned slightly to look at the injured boy he had spoken with just moments before, he realised that the boy had quietly died beside them. Nurse Flowers tried to control her tears, yet again.

'At least he didn't die alone, Chaplain.'

Sister Mackintosh, observing the sad scene, took both Chaplain and Nurse by their arms. She was uncharacteristically quiet.

'Come away now, Chaplain, and Nurse Flowers. Let the orderlies do their work. We have worked out a better plan for the allocation of space between the patients.'

Crispen Honeybourn couldn't rest until he had paid a visit to his burgeoning makeshift chapel. He was disappointed that he could not tell which sailors were Catholics and which were Anglicans, or any other faith. He adopted an ecumenical approach and recited the Lord's Prayer over them all before he allowed himself to go in search of a warm drink.

Everyone was exhausted. They had worked through the night without food or drink until it was almost dawn.

As the hospital ship moved slowly away from the bay, Crispen offered his thanks to Almighty God that they had survived the night.

'Here, Nurse Mabel, I've brought you a warm drink at last. I'm sorry I couldn't manage to find any milk.'

Mabel gave Crispen a tense half-smile, as much to express her relief that the situation seemed calmer, if still potentially fraught with danger.

'Thank you, Chaplain,' she said. 'I'm sure I will not notice the lack of milk in my tea. I must drink it before Sister Mackintosh does her rounds again. She might accuse me of slacking.'

'Come, Mabel, may I use your first name? I'll call you that when Sister Mackintosh isn't around. Mabel nodded, but this time she gave him a broader, more relaxed and confident smile.

'Yes, of course, Chaplain.'

'It's Crispen, please, Mabel.'

'All right, but only when Sister is not around.'

Crispen led Mabel to the survivors who were beginning to rouse from their troubled night of broken sleep and worry.

'Come, Mabel, I have an idea.'

Crispen had discovered that they were woefully out of tin mugs and proper cups, but had found a tray of small teapots.

'Some of the men would be able to drink tea through the spouts, if we help them steady the teapots.'

'What a brilliant idea.' Mabel enlisted the help of orderlies and some of the other nurses. The less seriously injured men were grateful for anything to drink at all, even water, should they happen to run out of tea.

The tea trays were shared out between the nurses and the orderlies. The less seriously injured patients were able to sip through the teapot spouts. Most of them could utter their thanks and even manage a sort of smile.

Mabel Flowers was glad to be doing something useful for the injured but suddenly recoiled in horror when faced with some of the more serious injuries.

'I thought I was becoming used to the sight of men who had lost limbs,' she confided to Crispen, 'but I am finding it difficult to deal with cases like this poor man.'

Mabel's hands were shaking as she bent down to offer the man some small sips. The man was shaking too.

'His face is almost completely swathed in bandages. I can't see his eyes and there is just a small opening for his mouth. Crispen, don't think he can hear me or even see. He also has two broken legs.'

Crispen took the small teapot from Mabel and helped her to her feet. She was close to tears. She wiped her face.

'Here, let me try. May I?'

Crispen offered the tea to the man. The patient swallowed just a few drops and gave a very slight nod of his head in thanks.

'Can you hear me?' Crispen asked the patient gently.

There was no further response.

'He has taken a few more drops. We'll try again later.'

Even the shyest of nurses became used to washing men's bodies and dressing wounds, though it seemed relentless and back-breaking work.

'What is more difficult,' Mabel explained to Crispen, 'is trying to calm their distress, especially when they scream out from their sleep. The nightmares must be horrific for them, as well as the awful pain.'

Crispen Honeybourn also had to admit that he felt shivers down his spine when he tried to help men through their mental agonies. He was being tested to the limits of his capabilities. He felt inadequate. He was better caring for the dead. He was there for them when no relative could be. He tried to give them as decent and beautiful a burial as if they were in their own home town. Sadly, he had now lost count of how many land and sea burials he had arranged. Sometimes, during the sea burials he had been momentarily lost for what he considered the right words. The standard texts and prayers seemed completely inappropriate. How could he speak of a merciful God in the face of such evil and carnage? Neither could he bring himself to acknowledge the notion of the glory of war.

Sister Marjorie Mackintosh soon jerked Crispen Honeybourn out of his low mood, with her no-nonsense manner.

'There you are, Chaplain. I am afraid we will have to call on you for more sea burials, at first light.'

Sister Mackintosh escorted her Chaplain back to his makeshift chapel where he found his newest charges. The group of new young nurses were awaiting him in the dark chapel area.

'We've prepared the bodies as decently as we could, Chaplain. The pity is that we do not have all their names. No proper records, you understand. In some cases, we have picked men up from different ships. Those who can speak don't always recognise the men beside them.'

'Fear not,' Chaplain Honeybourn reassured them.

'I will do my very best.'

Just before dawn broke, Crispen Honeybourn left the burial party for a few minutes in order to get some fresh air and to collect his own private thoughts. The nurses were exhausted and were trying to have a few minutes' sleep wherever they could find a space to lay their heads. Most of them were in the biggest state of shock they would ever experience in their lives. Coming face-to-face with the reality of war made all of them confront the limitations of their nursing skills, as well as the notion of honour and glory.

'It isn't just a case of bandaging wounds, is it, Sister?'

'No, Chaplain, it certainly isn't.'

Sister Mackintosh had followed Crispen to get some air herself. She seemed to be in a more affable and talkative mood just then, so Crispen dared to address her directly, and personally.

'Tell me, Sister, how do you manage to cope with all this stress and the relentless physical side of nursing in this situation?'

Crispen had no idea of what response he might get from Sister Mackintosh. She usually had little conversation, other than giving instructions.

'Me?'

Sister Mackintosh was surprised to be asked anything about herself.

'Oh! Sister. Please forgive me if that was too personal.'

'No, not at all,' she replied.

'I've always had to be tough,' she explained. 'My father and mother both died in an influenza epidemic when I was fifteen. I had to look after seven brothers and sisters. We managed with a bit of help from the parish. There was no time for tears and tantrums then – we just had to get on with it. We all had our jobs to do around the house. We worked out a work rota so we swapped the jobs around. Some of the children earned pennies from doing odd jobs for other people.'

'It must have been very hard for you, Sister?'

'Not as hard as this, Sir.'

Sister Mackintosh had very little sleep that night. Although she could appear to be very strict with her young, often inexperienced nurses, she recognised when they were at their wits' end. She could not afford for any of them to collapse before their work was done. She tried to encourage them to sleep as much as they possibly could.

Mabel was thankful that Sister Mackintosh had seemed less of a bully after her chat with Crispen. Sister Mackintosh did have a compassionate nature after all. Mabel was warming to her a little, but she was under no illusions that Sister Mackintosh's demeanour could change in a flash.

As dawn broke after that terrible, frightening night, the Chaplain and a small group of nurses, together with some of the ship's officers, formed a burial party. The dignified group stood towards the stern of the ship, away from the view of the injured men who would then be awake.

Some of the nurses stood stony-faced, determined not to cry. Others couldn't help themselves.

Sister Mackintosh volunteered to read a short prayer, and then, quite unscripted she addressed the small congregation.

'They did their duty. Now they have gone to join the friends who went before them. They would be happy to know they are together.'

Crispen Honeybourn did what was expected of him. He knew there would be many such occasions to come. He wouldn't buckle under the enormity of it, nor the feelings of senselessness of such horror all around them.

The hospital ship and the barges moved slowly away from the straits over the next few days. It would take a week or even more as they called at the Greek Islands on their zig-zag journey to Malta. The beautiful sunsets around the islands gave everyone a brief, though false sense of peace, for a time. Some of the nurses watched as the Chaplain blessed the men who were being transferred to smaller ships.

'They will be taken to hospitals on the islands, or to Malta,' Sister Mackintosh explained. 'I guess the luckiest ones will go back to England, probably to Plymouth.'

'What about Crispen? Where will he be sent, Sister?'

'Crispen, is it?'

Sister Mackintosh raised her eyebrows.

'Sorry, Sister, I mean Chaplain Honeybourn.'

Sister Mackintosh gave Mabel a very questioning look. She wondered if she had missed something meaningful.

'Actually, Nurse Flowers, I'm not sure where any of us will go.'

Mabel felt very uneasy, but she thanked Sister Mackintosh and moved away. The patient who was almost completely covered in bandages needed her attention. He was beginning to stir.

'Can I bring you anything?' she asked the patient.

There was no response. Mabel couldn't really tell for sure if he had heard her, or even if he could see properly through the small eye slits in his bandage.

'Sister! Sister!' she shouted.

'What's the shouting about, Nurse Flowers?'

'Sorry, Sister. This patient is trying to move for the first time. I'm not sure whether he can hear me, or if he can see.'

'I will see if the doctor is free to take a look at him. We must not move the bandages until we are told to do so. He may have very serious facial wounds. He could need surgery and I guess that will be better served at the Malta hospital in Mtarfa.'

Mabel shivered.

'I will try him with some tea, Sister, or do you think he might take some soup off a spoon?'

Sister Mackintosh bent down so that she could see the man's eyes.

'Now then, young sir, would you like some soup?'

They waited for an answer but the man didn't speak. Mabel thought he had blinked his eyes, as though to say 'Yes'. She repeated Sister Mackintosh's words.

'Soup!' Would you like some soup?'

This time the man gave the very briefest of nods with his head. Nurse Flowers smiled at the patient and touched his hand gently.

'Well done,' she said.

As yet, the man who couldn't or wouldn't speak was, of necessity, only known by the number which had been hastily stuck on to his chest as he had been rescued from the sea. He was Patient 355.

'Ah, yes! Patient 355,' the Medical Officer confirmed. 'Some of his fellow sailors will be sent to Imbros or Lemnos. This man needs to see the surgeons at Malta.'

Sister Mackintosh and Nurse Flowers watched anxiously as the ship's senior doctor attempted to remove the bandages from Patient 355. Inch by inch and very slowly he cut away tiny pieces of the caked-on dressing.

'That's all I dare to cut away for now,' the doctor explained. 'It's stuck good and hard to his entire face. In one sense, it might help protect him until we reach Malta.'

'Is that where he's going then, Doctor?'

'Yes, Sister. It's the best place for him. They have very good operating facilities there.'

'I understand the General hospitals on Imbros and Lemnos are full to capacity, Doctor.'

'That's what I have heard too, Sister. Anyhow I am not prepared to send this man to the Australian tent hospital. He needs specialist attention.'

Chaplain Honeybourn joined the group.

'Has he spoken yet, Sister?'

'Not a word, just a very slight nod.'

The doctor spent some time scrutinising the records of Patient 355. He expressed concern that the man was not making any kind of effort to speak. The Chaplain assured the doctor that every effort was being made to help the man.

'I have created more space around the patient's eyes and mouth, Sister. He should feel more comfortable. He should be able to take a little soft food. I suggest plenty of fluids as well.'

With that the doctor moved quickly on to deal with other cases which were giving cause for concern. He left instructions with Sister Mackintosh that should Patient 355 begin to speak she was to report it to the Senior Medical Officer immediately.

'Crikey, Sister. The doctor seemed very serious.'

'Well, I think we are in a very serious and worrying war. The man may very well be able to give military people more details of what happened to him. For all we know he could even be a German.'

Chaplain Honeybourn intervened immediately after hearing Sister Mackintosh hypothesising.

'Oh, no, Sister. I can assure you that he is definitely not a German sailor. He is certainly British. He is very deeply traumatised by what happened to him and he has no memory at present. He has very falteringly said one word to me. It was only a whisper, but it was audible.'

'What did he say, Chaplain?'

'He said "thanks" though it was a very soft whisper. It does mean that he has only lost his memory, not his reason.'

The doctor left Patient 355 in the care of the nurses. They were to take it in turns to sit by the patient until he made any verbal response at all.

'Report any changes to me immediately,' Sister Mackintosh addressed the group of nurses and orderlies, before hurrying on to accompany the doctor on his final rounds before the patients who were being moved off the ship were fully documented.

'Sister says when these men have been moved we will have much more room. It will give us a chance to thoroughly disinfect and scrub everywhere. The stench is unbelievable. It's a wonder we aren't all seriously ill.'

Mabel wiped her brow with her own now grey-looking handkerchief. She was ashamed to notice how dirty it had become. Crispen Honeybourn comforted her, then changed the subject.

'I wonder if we will take on extra patients from the islands?'

'I think Sister said there were some serious surgical cases.

She doubted whether some of them would survive another sea journey.'

Sister Mackintosh returned to the ward. She looked relieved to have seen the doctor depart.

'It can't be much longer now,' Sister Mackintosh said in an anguished voice. 'I, for one, will be overjoyed to reach Malta and walk on terra firma again!'

The assembled group of nurses and orderlies heartily agreed, but laughed out loud at Sister Mackintosh's turn of phrase.

The ward orderlies set about disinfecting and scrubbing every possible surface. The nurses cleaned the remaining patients, and Nurse Mabel Flowers found a way of disposing of her 'shameful' handkerchief.

She longed for the time when she would be back in England, in a nice clean hospital and with bright, starched aprons. She had not realised just how much would be a case of improvising and making-do with the facilities and equipment to hand on a hospital ship. It wasn't like a conventional, ordered hospital. So much could change by the hour, and certainly by the day. She suddenly felt very homesick.

Sister Mackintosh gathered her nurses together for her rounds of the remaining patients. She stopped by each bed and described as well as she could the details of each man's condition. Chaplain Honeybourn followed on behind with his notebook. He had his own way of writing shorthand notes. He was sure to be asked to identify patients when they arrived in Malta. Some were still without names, but he would try his best to glean whatever information he could. Mostly he liked to talk with the patients themselves.

The entourage arrived at the bedside of Patient 355.

'This poor man has serious facial injuries and two broken legs. The doctor thinks his legs will heal in time. They cannot give a clear prognosis about his face until all the bandages come off. Sadly, he still appears to be deeply traumatised and cannot speak. He can see us through his bandages, though we cannot tell whether he can hear us.'

Crispen Honeybourn thought that the man had tried to thank him and that he had given a very slight, nervous nod when he was offered tea.

'Of course, it may just have been the light which startled him, but I was sure that he had tried to nod his thanks.'

'Would you allow me some time with him, Sister? Alone?'

'Very well, Chaplain, but not too long. Send for help if he proves to be troublesome.'

Troublesome, Crispen thought to himself. The man was clearly in deep shock still. He stared vacantly as if he was somewhere else, somewhere strange, and far far away.

Sister Mackintosh continued her rounds, but Mabel Flowers held back.

'Crispen, please let me help. Sister Mackintosh means well, though she can be quite brusque at times.'

'You seem to be getting on better with her now, Mabel.'

'Yes, I am beginning to understand her better. She has taught me a lot about nursing. There are some horrific cases. I realise we cannot run away from the awful things we see here. They have to be dealt with as carefully and efficiently as we can manage. I'm learning to develop a more positive attitude and a tougher personality. It isn't about *my* feelings, is it?'

'What a very lovely and wise young nurse you are, Mabel Flowers.'

Mabel smiled, then blushed as she realised that Crispen was holding her hands. He planted a gentle kiss on each of her hands then they both sat down beside Patient 355.

Crispen looked into the man's eyes and smiled.

'Can you hear me?' There was no immediate response. Crispen paused and then tried again.

'If you can hear me, please can you blink your eyes twice?'

The man stared at Crispen and then blinked slowly twice.

'Crispen, you did it!'

Mabel was filled with admiration and praise for both Crispen and Patient 355. She ran off to tell Sister Mackintosh that the man had responded. The Sister hurried back to see for herself.

'It was just a couple of blinks, Sister,' Mabel said, 'it was when Crispen… er… , sorry, Sister. It was when Chaplain Honeybourn spoke to him and asked him to blink twice if he could hear him.'

'Excellent work, Chaplain. Has he spoken yet?'

'Thank you, Sister. No, he hasn't spoken yet. I will continue to encourage him.'

Sister Mackintosh regaled them with stories of what was being termed 'shell-shock'.

'Some of these poor men just stared all the time, appearing as though they were in some kind of trance, in another world entirely. Some had violent dreams and woke up screaming. We've let the worst case go to Lemnos this time. They have an Australian doctor there who is an expert in dealing with such cases. I'm not sure if Mtarfa hospital will have such a specialist. We will soon find out.'

'Couldn't we have let this man off to Lemnos, Sister?'

'We could have, Chaplain, but his face and legs are in need of surgical operations. Malta will serve him best.'

Sister Mackintosh thought that the man's physical wounds would heal, in time. As for is mental state, no one could tell. Perhaps when he returned to England he might find help with his mental state.

'You see, young nurses,' the Sister continued, 'mental trauma like this is a fairly new problem for the doctors. They might be sympathetic, but do not always have the means to cure them.'

Crispen Honeybourn added his experience to the topic of conversation.

'I have seen men, mostly land soldiers who had been shot at, or deafened by explosions, being treated very badly by their officers. Some were accused of being cowards, when actually they were severely shocked and frightened… '

Mabel Flowers decided to change the mood and the conversation.

'Sister, would it be all right if we were to try and bathe the patient. Well, those bits of him that aren't bandaged?'

Sister Mackintosh hesitated as she took a long hard look at the man.

'We will certainly have to try and bathe him before we arrive in Malta. We won't have time in the morning. We dock quite early.'

Sister Mackintosh summoned two more nurses to help. Nurse Annie Vidler and Nurse Mary Wilson came to help. They wheeled the bath trolley nearer to the bed. It was just a small tin bath mounted on a trolley so that it could easily be moved between patients.

'You may just find it easier to bathe the man while he is in the bed. His feet are a dreadful mess, but we may not be able to move his splinted legs. He is in such a poor state we must make him feel more comfortable before we reach Mtarfa hospital.'

Patient 355 allowed the three nurses to gently bathe his arms and hands and however little of his bandaged face they could reach. He didn't flinch as they washed slowly around his upper body.

'Now for the legs,' said Mabel. 'Look, you two hold his legs out straight, over the side of the bed. I will wash around the splints and his feet.'

'Gently does it!'

They tried to explain to the patient what they intended to do next, but as they held his legs out over the side of the bed he caught sight of the water in the bath. His vacant stare became a look of absolute horror. He screamed.

'No! No! Help me, Charlie.'

Sister Mackintosh and the Chaplain came running as fast as they could when they heard the man's piercing cries.

Crispen Honeybourn took complete control of the situation. He took a towel from one of the nurses and held it against the man's face until he could be manoeuvred safely back on to the bed.

'Lay him down, back on the pillow, Nurse.'

Crispen spoke softly to the patient.

'There, you are quite safe now. Just close your eyes and rest.'

The patient continued to sob intermittently, but with Crispen holding his hand, he eventually quietened. The nurses took away the portable bath and moved away from the ward to leave the two men in peace.

Nurse Flowers kept peering back towards Crispen and the patient.

'He won't let go of the face towel, Sister. He's holding it up to cover his face.'

'Come away now, Nurse. Let the Chaplain deal with him.'

Crispen sat beside the man all night long, holding his hand

'Just relax, now. You are safe now. Sleep if you can.'

Crispen wondered if he should have said that. What if they weren't safe? There was every chance that another enemy torpedo might come their way. Still, he reasoned, the nearer they were to Malta, the safer they would all feel.

Sister Mackintosh returned several hours later.

'Have you been here all night, Chaplain? Can I bring you a drink?'

'No, thank you, Sister. I'm fine. I just feel pretty useless. I am not a doctor. All I can do is to try and calm him down. It's easier if they can talk, of course.'

'Aye, there's a good few more in the next bay in a similar situation. We think a few are from *HMS Goliath*. Others were picked up from other ships. We might even have some enemy troops here!'

Crispen Honeybourn looked startled.

'I expect we won't know who any of them are until they can speak about their ordeal.'

Crispen, ashen-faced, agreed.

'I expect many of the rescued men will have been randomly plucked from the sea, and in a hurry, for fear of more torpedoes?'

Sister Mackintosh nodded.

'We will be in Malta in just a few hours. Try to get some sleep Chaplain Honeybourn.'

'Thank you, Sister. I will just sit here beside him and I'll probably manage forty winks. I want to be here if he wakes.'

Sister Mackintosh brought a blanket and placed it carefully around the Chaplain's shoulders. She patted him.

'There, that's better, isn't it?'

Nurse Mabel, Nurse Annie and Nurse Mary talked quietly together, and huddled in a quiet corner of the ward, covering themselves with blankets. They were all exhausted but couldn't sleep properly. Each of them wondering and worrying what the morning would bring.

'It's scary, but exciting at the same time,' said one.

''Ere, did you see that?' Annie whispered.

'See what?'

'Sister Mackintosh putting a blanket over the Chaplain. Ever so careful she was.'

Mabel explained that the Chaplain had opted to sit by the shell-shocked patient until morning.

'He's quiet now, thank goodness. Poor man.'

Annie wasn't going to let the tittle-tattle drop.

'I reckon that Sister Mackintosh fancies Crispen Honeybourn. What do you think girls?'

Mary found it impossible to stifle her giggles.

'She could call him Honeybun, couldn't she?'

Then all three of them giggled.

'Shut up, you lot!'

One of the patients had heard the three nurses giggling.

'You'll wake everyone up if you ain't careful, at least those of us who ain't on the morphine.'

The three nurses, suitably chastised and ashamed, crept away to find another corner where they could grab some sleep. They were supposed to be on duty, but they took it in turns, an hour on and an hour off. They would certainly need all their strength, and their wits about them when dawn broke.

The hospital ship, surrounded by several other smaller craft, had made its way slowly into the harbour. Sister Mackintosh was quick to take charge.

'Come on, nurses. Don't loiter. We have a lot of work to do.'

The nurses followed her, glimpsing for the first time the coastline of Malta. It was dazzling in the morning sun.

'Isn't Malta beautiful, Sister?'

'I dare say it is, Nurse Vidler. You'll have time to admire it later.'

'Come along, nurses, I need you to assist the orderlies. We must make sure that every patient has the correct casualty label pinned on his chest.'

'We can't put a name on this one, Sister. He can't tell us his name.'

Annie was pointing to Patient 355, who hadn't spoken a word yet, save for him screaming the name 'Charlie' when they tried to bathe him.

'Is your name Charlie?' Annie asked the man.

The man tried to say 'No' but the sound wouldn't come from his lips. He became more and more anxious and agitated as he was taken on a stretcher to be transferred to a barge bound for the Mtarfa hospital ashore.

'Well, he will just have to go with his number. You will accompany him Nurse Flowers.'

Sister Mackintosh explained the plans to the nurses. The patients would be assessed by the ship's doctors. Those deemed fit enough to join hospital trains would be sent back to England. Those who weren't would receive treatment on one of the islands. The serious cases would be sent to Malta hospitals.

'Lucky blighters, if they're going home,' said Annie.

'I'm not so sure they feel lucky, exactly,' Mabel answered.

Annie lowered her voice so that Sister Mackintosh wouldn't hear.

'I wish I was going home. I wish I'd never come.'

'Annie Vidler! How could you?!' Mabel whispered.

'We're all trying to do our bit,' Mary chipped in, 'even if it wasn't exactly our job of choice. Just think of all the ones we've saved. Besides, we might be going home soon ourselves.'

'Well, Nurse Wilson. You'll be accompanying some patients to Lemnos, before you see England again.'

'Oh! Sister!' pouted Annie Vidler. 'I thought we would all be together.'

'Don't be so silly, Nurse Vidler. You have to go where you are most needed. It isn't my decision. The doctors have decided who is needed where.'

With their instructions given and only a short time to bid farewell to Mary, the other two nurses gathered their belongings together and made their way to the exit points.

'Never mind, Mary,' Annie shouted after them. 'Just think, you'll be looking after some of those strapping Australian soldiers. We've got to put up with Sister Mackintosh!'

'Yes, but you've got Crispen as well. It's not fair!!'

Crispen had found his way into all their hearts, though he was quite oblivious to all their girlish banter.

The three friends hugged each other. Mabel could hardly be heard above the noise and throng surrounding them. It seemed as though the entire ship's company were disembarking.

'We'll all meet up in London when it's all over,' she shouted.

Crispen was assigned to remain with Patient 355 on his journey to the specialist unit at Mtarfa hospital.

'It will be more peaceful for him there, won't it, Sister?'

'I hope so, Chaplain. I am not sure whether they can cope with the patient's mental state. We have yet to find out.'

'Yes, quite, Sister. I have been warned that there may be many such cases there already. I guess the physical injuries will be dealt with first.'

Sister Mackintosh nodded. The two of them stood quietly and watched anxiously as more and more of the hospital patients were being moved. None of the nurses, including Sister Mackintosh knew, exactly where they would be billeted once they had arrived in Malta.

'It could be that we are all separated,' the Sister said, 'but I hope not.'

She threw a wistful glance in the Chaplain's direction.

'I really would like to know how our mystery patient progresses. You will let me know, Chaplain, won't you?'

'Of course I will, Sister. I am sure that Mtarfa is not so large that we won't be able to find each other. Of course, I may very well be shipped off somewhere else, who knows? I'm only with you by default!'

Nurse Annie Vidler smirked mischievously.

'There!' she whispered to Mabel. 'Did you see the look she gave him?'

'Shut up, Annie.'

Mabel nudged her friend in the back.

'You'd better behave yourself now. There won't be so many places to hide as there are on the ship. Believe me, Sister Mackintosh will be looking out for you.'

'For us both, you mean. I think Sister Mackintosh is envious of your friendship with Crispen Honeybun!'

'Stop it! Stop it, Annie!'

Her friend giggled.

'You mustn't call him that, even in jest. One day you will forget it's a bit of fun and call him that by mistake.'

Patient 355 was being carefully lifted on to a secure stretcher. He became agitated as he tried to peer through his face bandages.

'Don't worry, chum,' said the orderly. 'Me and my mate Cyril are going to stay with you until you are safe on land and in your nice clean hospital bed with all those lovely nurses looking after you.'

Mabel kept a close eye on the three of them.

'Should we cover his face as he's leaving the ship?' she asked Sister Mackintosh, anxiously.

'It might be a good idea, Nurse, but he will have to face the water sooner or later.'

'Of course, Sister. It's just that he is likely to have another panic attack as he's being moved onto the smaller ship.'

Sister Mackintosh decided that the patient should have a sedative.

'What's your name, chum?' the orderly asked.

The patient shook his head.

'He can't remember,' Mabel said. 'He has had such a bang to

his head that he has lost his memory. Sister told us that he might get it back when the wounds heal.'

'It's funny though,' Annie chipped into the conversation. 'When we tried to use the trolley-bath he seemed to have some kind of flashback. He couldn't face the water and he shouted for someone called Charlie.'

Sister Mackintosh returned with the sedative.

The orderly gently asked the patient if he could remember who Charlie was. The man looked puzzled and shook his head. He took the sedative from Sister Mackintosh, then turned away from them, covering himself with the sheet.

'Okay, chum. Never mind. Let's get you out of here. You have a snooze all the way. It'll do you good.'

'What will happen to him, Sister?' Mabel asked.

'I expect he'll be assessed for his physical injuries first. Then the doctors will decide if they can help his mental state. There are many more of such cases. It's what they call shell-shock, or depression.'

'Will he recover?'

'I don't know, Nurse Flowers. We have to wait and see.'

Sister Mackintosh turned to move away to her other tasks, but she turned back for a few moments to caution the nurses.

'You must concentrate on the task you are given. Try not to become emotional or attached to any of your charges. The job is hard enough.'

'We all understand that, Sister.'

Surprisingly, Sister Mackintosh seemed to have suddenly mellowed.

'You are a promising young nurse, Mabel Flowers. I expect you might go far. Try not to let Nurse Vidler sidetrack you. I'm hoping that you will be a good influence on her!'

'Yes, Sister. Thank you. I will do my best.'

The Sister left them to assist the orderlies to move Patient 355 on his tricky journey across the bay and into the harbour, towards the peace of a proper hospital bed.

They reached dry land without any mishaps, but their arrival at the hospital was initially anything but peaceful. Patients being moved this way and that, soldiers shouting, and nurses in a state of real frustration. Hardly any of them knew where they were needed.

'It's big, ain't it?!' gasped Annie. 'There's workmen all over the place. Are you sure we're in the right place, Mabel?'

'We are in the right place, Annie. It will feel different now. It'll be soldiers, not sailors, telling us what to do and where to go. Soldiers shout louder too!'

Part Two

The arrival of many more injured soldiers together with their nurses and orderlies was chaotic. New wards had to be hastily improvised and existing ones adapted to take even more beds. Even cupboards were being ripped out to provide basic treatment areas. Mabel Flowers and Annie Vidler joined their group of new nurses. They were twenty nervous young women. They had all volunteered without realising how horrendously shocking and tiring their work would be.

'Come along, nurses. Follow me!'

They heard the voice of the Chaplain.

'Oh, it's Crispen, Mabel.'

'Thank goodness, a friendly face, Annie.'

The Chaplain's first order was to escort the group of new nurses to their accommodation. They were to be billeted for the time being in a converted barrack block, away from the hospital wards and away from the ANZAC troops who had begun to arrive.

'I say, Mabel. It's a bit primitive, ain't it?'

'At least it's clean, Annie. We've got curtains 'round our beds.'

'Where's the privvy?' another nurse asked desperately. 'I need to go NOW!'

Just then Sister Mackintosh caught up with the group.

'You've arrived at last, thank goodness. You must all thank Chaplain Honeybourn for escorting you safely here.'

'Thank you, Chaplain Honeybourn,' they chorused, trying to mimic Sister Mackintosh's accent.

Annie did forget herself and was scolded by Mabel for calling the Chaplain 'Honeybun'.

'It's a good job Sister didn't hear you say that. If you say it again, Annie, I shan't talk to you any more.'

'I think I'll marry a sailor when we get out of here,' Annie vowed. 'What about you, Mabel?'

'What!? Marry a sailor, no fear. They'd never be at home. I wouldn't marry a soldier either.'

'I expect you'd like to marry someone like Crispen Honeybun?'

Mabel was annoyed and chased her friend to their first designated hospital block.

'I've told you not to say that,' Mabel said crossly.

They were like a couple of silly schoolgirls one minute and then suddenly everything changed.

The group of fresh-faced eager young nurses watched as their Chaplain disappeared from their view. His official duties called as he dealt with funerals, one after the other. The hospital complex was near to the Royal Navy cemetery, Sister Mackintosh explained.

'We will become used to seeing many such funerals.'

'Are these our men, Sister, or are they Australian troops?'

The nurses fell silent as Sister Mackintosh spoke in hushed tones, for once.

'They will be Australians, New Zealanders and British.'

Sister Mackintosh and the nurses walked in silence to their new wards at Mtarfa hospital. Most of the young nurses had very little idea of what the war was about or who was who. They volunteered for a myriad of reasons with all the innocence and energy of youth, at least in the beginning. Seeing the injured sailors rescued from the straits had been shocking enough, but the injuries sustained by the land troops seemed even worse. One of the junior doctors tried to explain it to the nurses.

'What you need to remember is that some of these men were not only injured, but often left in the hot, searing sun for many hours before they were found and brought to safety.'

The mood was sombre. All frivolity had been forgotten as the nurses began the work they had volunteered to do.

Row upon row of makeshift beds were closely packed together. Each had a number and a code to show whether the bed's occupant was mildly injured, seriously injured, or beyond help.

'Nurse Flowers, you can begin here with the bathing routine before the doctors begin their next rounds.'

Sister Mackintosh pointed to the first row of mildly injured patients. Mabel was relieved.

'Some will talk and joke with you,' Sister warned. 'Just ignore them if their language becomes a bit rich.'

Mabel raised her eyebrows and Annie Vidler giggled. She was remembering how 'rich' her father's language could be when he had imbibed too much liquor.

'Come with me, Nurse Vidler. For now, I want you to work with Nurse Bell. She is less experienced. I hope you will show her what to do.'

'Yes, Sister. I'll do my best.'

Annie was more than a little anxious as she was directed to the more poorly patients.

'Come on then, Nurse Bell,' she encouraged her new assistant. 'Follow me. What's your first name?'

'Betty, Miss. Betty Bell.'

'Blimey, I'm not a Miss. Well, I mean strictly speaking I am Miss Vidler, but you can call me Annie. If we call each other just "Nurse" we'll none of us know who the other is, and anyhow first names are more friendly – except for Sister Mackintosh. She goes by her proper name and she calls everyone by their proper names, so you are Nurse Bell.'

'How old are you, Betty?'

'I'm seventeen, Miss, I mean, Annie.'

Annie doubted that Nurse Betty Bell was actually seventeen, but she didn't challenge her. Betty Bell seemed little more than a child. She was very thin and pale, possibly under-nourished, Annie guessed. When Annie was introduced to Betty her eyes were red with crying. Sister Mackintosh had insisted that Betty's very long, plaited hair be cut short.

'It's hard enough for all of us to stay clean in this place,' Sister Mackintosh had told her, 'and we mustn't waste water. Besides, that long hair would always get in the way of your work.'

'It'll soon grow back, Betty,' Annie tried to sympathise.

When they were free of Sister Mackintosh's eyes they took a slow walk around their many sick charges.

'Are these men mildly injured, Annie?'

'It's a matter of comparisons, see,' Annie replied.

She stopped to talk to one of the patients so that Betty would learn how to speak to them.

'Hello, I'm Nurse Vidler. May I read your doctor's notes?'

The soldier nodded but was reluctant to speak. Annie glanced at the notes even though she couldn't understand most of the medical terms. She did make out the word 'amputation'. She held her breath and then very carefully replaced the notes at the side of the soldier's bed.

'Thank you,' she said, trying to sound like Sister Mackintosh.

'Are they going to cut it off tomorrow?' the soldier asked.

Annie became worried and not a little panic-stricken. She knew that she shouldn't have read the notes because now she didn't know whether the doctors had discussed the matter with the soldier, or not. It was not her place to reveal anything that she had read. She had merely been trying to make the new nurse, Betty Bell, feel more confident about talking with patients. Betty, noticing Annie's hesitation, stepped in quite quickly.

'Here, let me straighten your pillow,' she said to the soldier. 'You'll feel much more comfortable if you lie back on it, won't you? That's it, lie back and have a snooze till Sister comes.'

The soldier half smiled and laid back. Annie took her new nurse by the arm as they moved away from the soldier's bed.

'Well, Betty Bell! What a surprise you are. You're a shy little thing, hardly daring to open your mouth to anyone. Then you behave perfectly with the patient, as though you have been doing it for years.'

'I have, Miss. I mean, Annie. I had to nurse my father through his illness. He died of consumption, the doctor said. Before that my mother caught the Spanish flu in the epi— epidem—'

'Epidemic,' Annie helped her to remember the correct word.

'I am so sorry to hear that, Betty. What a dreadful time you have had. Did you have anyone to help you?'

'There was my brother, Will. He's fifteen now. He's joined the army now. The other kids had to go to relatives. They're too young to look after themselves.'

'Gracious, Betty, how many were there?'

'Four others. My two younger brothers have gone to my Mum's cousin, Ellice. She stands no nonsense. She's very strict. They have to go to school. The two girls are with a school teacher and her husband, so they will be all right. They have a girl of their own called Rose.'

'So how did you decide to become a volunteer nurse, Betty?'

Betty's answer just then seemed to convince Annie that perhaps Betty hadn't lied about her age.

'Well, cousin Ellice used to be a nurse and I sort of got talked into it. She's working for a lady politician and she's a suffrager – or something like that.'

'A suffragette?'

'That's it. I'm not sure what they do. She's not at home much, the boys tell me. You see, Annie, if I had stayed at home with them I would have just carried on being a servant for the rest of my life. I know that sounds awful of me, but I thought it was for the best.'

'Well, frail little Betty – Nurse Betty Bell. You have got a good head on you, as my old mother used to say. I don't think you are awful at all. I think you will make a fine nurse.'

Betty gave her a smile for once, and the soldier she had spoken to a few minutes before shouted after her.

'You've a nice smile, Nurse.'

Sister Mackintosh was looming nearby so Annie hurried Betty along.

'We'd better get a move on, Betty, or we'll be in trouble.'

Betty, feeling more confident now with Annie by her side, couldn't stop chattering.

'My Ma used to have lots of sayings too. She used to say you shouldn't look down on anybody unless you are prepared to help them up.'

'Did your mother go to church, Betty?'

'We all did. She was very keen on it. I liked the singing. The singing was good. I can remember all the words of the hymns, even if I didn't always understand what they meant.'

That night in their billet, the group of new nurses had begun to relax and quite soon were beginning to feel more comfortable in each other's company. They had all had an exhausting day and were anxious of what the next day might bring.

They chattered well into the night until one by one they began to fall asleep. Betty Bell was the only nurse of the group who felt quite comfortable kneeling on the floor beside her bed. She had been taught to say her prayers every night. It was the natural thing to do. She would pray for them all.

'Dear Lord,' she whispered. 'Bless us all and keep us safe, even Sister Mackintosh and the Chaplain… oh and all the poorly sailors and soldiers. Please make the war end soon. Amen.'

Mabel and Annie had both observed Betty saying her prayers. Mabel was sure that whatever Betty's age was she was going to be fine. In fact, in some respects Betty seemed to be more mature than Annie Vidler. Annie was a very conscientious nurse and her heart was in the right place but on occasions she could be far too outspoken. Without really meaning to give offence, words sometimes came tumbling from her mouth in the wrong way. Mabel, who was blessed with more intuition than her new nurse friends, had learned to recognise things like Annie's raised eyebrows and mild protestations of 'what?' after she had been chided for her lack of tact. Mabel guessed it must have developed from Annie's childhood and living with brothers. She would always have had to fight her corner in any real arguments.

Despite having to sleep in yet more strange surroundings and in what could possibly be still fraught with danger, the nurses slept.

After morning ablutions in a temporary washing area, the nurses hurried to dress. Sister Mackintosh would inspect them as if they were soldier recruits. They were to have their hair covered and there was to be no trace of perfume of any kind.

'Good honest soap and water is all you need here,' Sister shouted as she walked up and down inspecting uniforms as well as hands and faces.

After breakfast the nurses would be assigned to their wards.

'Cor, it's like being a soldier on parade,' Annie complained.

'Stop moaning, Annie,' Mabel said. 'Look what a lovely bright morning it is – and look back there to the buildings near the harbour. See how they glisten.'

'They look pink, don't they?' Betty noticed.

Chaplain Honeybourn had caught up with the group as they went in search of the breakfast canteen.

'There are many beautiful old buildings here in Malta. They look pink in the sunshine because of the red sand which was brought from Africa.'

'Chaplain, how do you know all that history?'

Mabel was entranced.

'When things improve here I promise I will escort you ladies around Valletta and all the splendid churches. You must see the lovely paintings and carvings. They are truly magnificent.'

'Do you think we'll ever get time off, Chaplain?' asked Annie.

'We'll have to wait and see. I doubt you will be allowed to go out unescorted into the towns, not yet.'

When work began, Mabel, Annie, and young Betty were to be teamed up with two new nurses each. They were assigned to different wards. Annie complained that they wouldn't see each other again until their evening meal.

'It's so that we can show the new nurses around. Some of them have come straight from England and some have very little training,' Mabel explained.

'But we're new nurses too,' Betty added.

'You all have to help each other.'

Sister Mackintosh had appeared after inspecting all the new nurses. She gave each of them a written schedule of work.

'I can't be behind all of you at once, especially as we are being asked to take more and more patients every day. The eldest of each group will take charge and you must report anything you can't deal with to me immediately.'

'Yes, Sister,' they all chimed.

The first few weeks were indeed very chaotic. The injured and the sick patients came and went according to the severity of their condition. Some were patched up and eventually put on transport of one kind or another. Some found their places on hospital trains which took them on the long journey back to England. Some cases were to remain in Mtarfa. Patient 355 still needed to be X-rayed before he could be moved. It was possible that he may need surgery.

Chaplain Honeybourn spent time with Patient 355 each morning and again each night. He was there beside the man when he awoke from his frequently fitful, nightmarish sleep.

'Do you know me this morning?' he would gently ask the man.

Day by day he would ask the same question and, gradually, day by day the man nodded with more certainty.

Crispen didn't want to push the man too hard, but he waited for those moments when he seemed less agitated. Then he would venture to ask again whether he could remember his name. Sometimes the man just shook his head and then there were times when he became frustrated and tearful.

'Never mind, old chap,' Crispen reassured him. It may take a while, but I am sure you will recover your memory one day. Let the doctors mend your body first.'

Crispen's patient listened and he didn't flinch when Crispen took his hands in his and said a quiet prayer with him. It seemed to calm him down.

At night, when all was quiet on the ward, Crispen would return to sit beside Patient 355 as he struggled to go to sleep. No words were exchanged between them, but Crispen felt certain that simply by his being there, the man felt safer.

Sister Mackintosh did her rounds during the night and she would, more often than not, discover Chaplain Honeybourn had nodded off to sleep beside the patient. She would give him a gentle shake.

'Chaplain, you should leave him now. Go and have a proper sleep in your own quarters. You will have another taxing day tomorrow.'

The Chaplain would indeed have another harrowing day to come. There would be several more visits to the nearby cemetery. After that he had volunteered to accompany a group of nurses, together with several patients, to a larger, private hospital where they could be X-rayed. They would have to be transported in a rickety old army ambulance on the mile-long journey.

Soon after breakfast the patients were prepared for travel in the ambulance. Those who could be strapped in safely were placed in the motor ambulance first; the nurses and Crispen had to find a small corner for themselves and were advised to 'hang on'. The road was not entirely smooth.

The Medical Officer in charge of the X-ray Department expressed surprise at the new arrivals.

'Haven't you heard? We caught a couple of stray shells. The X-ray unit has been damaged. We will have to send you somewhere else.'

Mabel Flowers was in a quandary. What should she do? She was the Senior Nurse on that occasion. Crispen Honeybourn was not medically qualified to take the decision.

'It looks like the decision is up to you, Nurse Mabel.' Crispen said he would support whatever Mabel decided.

'Very well,' agreed Mabel. 'I don't think we really have a choice, but what about Sister Mackintosh?'

The Medical Officer assured them that the Maltese hospital would be expecting them and if he issued the order himself then it would, in case of emergency (as this was) be quite acceptable at their base unit. Sister Mackintosh would be informed.

'We'd better not delay then,' Mabel agreed.

Rather than feeling suddenly very senior, Nurse Mabel Flowers was feeling more than anxious. She was frightened. What if they

36

should encounter more stray enemy shells en route? What if the old, battered ambulance broke down? What if it took longer than anticipated and they were forced to find their way back to their base camp in the darkness?

Mabel need not have worried. They were expected at the new hospital and were received kindly. The patients were quickly whisked away to be X-rayed. Chaplain Honeybourn and the nurses were taken to a waiting room and provided with cups of tea. The place was sparkling clean and the Maltese nurses were pristine, friendly and most helpful.

'What a change from our hospital,' Mabel whispered.

'Yes it is, but don't forget, Mabel, this isn't a military hospital. It is a private, civilian hospital. It is very good of them to help us in the circumstances. In fact, Mabel, do you know that Malta has a long reputation throughout history for helping soldiers, knights even, when they were injured in war?'

Mabel didn't want to reveal her lack of knowledge so she just nodded.

'Let's just pray to God that this will all be over soon.'

The anxious nurses and their Chaplain waited patiently until the Maltese doctor appeared with news of their patients.

'Two of the men were quite straightforward,' he told them. They can return with you to your military base. I'm afraid we will have to keep your Patient 355. His fractures were a bit tricky. We have done the best we can and re-plastered him. He will need to be still for some days yet.'

Chaplain Honeybourn couldn't hide his concern and distress.

'This man is in deep shock, Doctor. He has lost his memory and he doesn't know his name or what has happened to him.'

'Don't worry,' the doctor assured him. 'We will take very good care of him. We will keep him quiet. If necessary we will sedate him, but I am confident that he will recover more quickly than you expect.'

'Can I come back to visit him?' the Chaplain asked.

'Yes, of course.'

The doctor offered Crispen his hand and Crispen thanked him.

With that assurance the nurses and their Chaplain went in search of their transport back to base camp.

'You're worried about leaving him, aren't you, Crispen?'

'Yes, Mabel, I am. I had just begun to feel that I was gaining the man's confidence. Now I fear he may relapse and sink even further into his depression.'

'Can't you stay with him for a few days,' she asked.

'Well, I would need special permission and that would also mean leaving the many dozens of other men I ought to be looking after, not to mention the inevitable funerals.'

'Are you the only chaplain on the base, Crispen?'

'I'm not sure yet. The place is quite vast and the numbers are growing all the time. There must be another chaplain or two, somewhere. The doctor here has told me that the Maltese have opened up some places as convalescent homes for the soldiers. One is in a gymnasium, another in Sliema has opened tea rooms as well. They are even putting concerts on for the troops.'

Suddenly the nurses were quite attentive.

'Who would give you special permission to stay here, Crispen?'

'I'm not quite sure, Mabel. I am here with sailors by accident. I was meant to be with the land forces at Gallipoli.'

'How did that happen, Chaplain?' asked Betty.

'I don't really know. Embarkation at the time was so chaotic. I just got pushed along in the throng of sailors. I didn't know which ship I was on at first.'

'Well, Chaplain, I am so glad you are here with us,' Betty said. Then she walked ahead to catch up with the other nurses.

Crispen Honeybourn walked with Mabel.

'I'm glad to be here with you Mabel, and the other nurses, of course. Isn't it strange how we are led down one path while fully expecting to follow another?'

'Do you really believe that we are led, Crispen, or are we truly masters of our own fate?'

'My word, Nurse Flowers, that sounds very deep indeed?'

Mabel thought carefully before she answered.

'Does that mean, Crispen, that you wouldn't expect a young, naive nurse such as myself to be capable of thinking so deeply?'

'Now you are embarrassing me, Mabel. I do apologise if I sounded a bit pompous.'

She smiled. It was then that her outward smile revealed much to Crispen about Mabel's inner thoughts.

Crispen Honeybourn was jolted back to reality. He worried about the man they had left behind. He urged the nurses to look for their transport back to base.

'I will go with the patient myself. I can't leave him. I will explain everything to Sister when I return. You will be safe with the driver and orderly.'

'But what if he needs, you know, personal stuff doing?'

'Don't you think about that. I will use one of the Maltese orderlies. I will need to do that in case I need to understand the language.'

'Most people can speak good English, sir,' one of the orderlies assured him.

The nurses were not happy at leaving their Chaplain to fend for himself, but they had little choice.

'I guess we'll be in for a telling-off when we get back,' Annie offered.

When the nurses arrived back at their initial base hospital they could hardly believe their eyes. It seemed as though hundreds more soldiers were streaming into the place, from a hospital ship which had been ordered to take a zig-zag route to fool the enemy.

'It's taken a week for us to get here, Nurse. We've hardly had a proper meal for days,' one soldier shouted.

'Are all these men injured?' asked Annie.

'Some are injured, Miss,' the soldier said. 'A lot of them have got dysentery and some have malaria.'

Nurses Mabel and Annie were quick to realise what a very serious situation they were in.

'We need to find Sister Mackintosh right away, Mabel.'

'No, no, we need to get ourselves cleaned up and find face masks. Some of these men will have to be isolated and we are rather unclean from travelling in the dusty ambulance. Just look at the numbers pouring in.'

Sister Mackintosh spotted the two nurses hurrying towards her.

'At last! Thank goodness you're back. We need you desperately. Where has Chaplain Honeybourn got to?'

Mabel started to explain how they'd had a very tiring and really frustrating journey, only to discover that the X-ray unit at the Malta hospital had been destroyed by a stray shell.

'They have taken Patient 355 to another private hospital to be X-rayed, Sister. The Chaplain has stayed with him. We were sent back.'

'Very well. Please go and get yourselves scrubbed up as fast as you can. I need you both in Ward A, on reception duties. The new girls are not much use to me yet. Nurse Flowers, I would like you to take charge until I can get back to you.'

'Yes, Sister. We're on our way.'

Sister Mackintosh hurried away to direct the orderlies. If she didn't keep an eye on them they would just keep on bringing more patients without there being any room to put them. They were forced to work all that day and through the night. Shifting patients who could be moved from beds to a mattress on the floor.

'This is far worse than the hospital ships.' Sister Mackintosh couldn't help expressing her sheer frustration to anyone who could spare a few seconds to listen.

'Nurse Flowers! Nurse Flowers!'

Nurse Flowers came running. She had never seen Sister in such a state as this. Her uniform was soiled with blood and her hair tangled as though it hadn't been brushed for days.

'Nurse Flowers, where is Chaplain Honeybourn?'

'I'm here, Sister. What can I do?'

'Where is Crispen – I mean Chaplain Crispen?'

'Don't you remember, Sister? He had to take Patient 355 to another hospital. We were sent back on our own because you were in need of us here.'

Sister Mackintosh looked dazed and she was on the verge of hysterical tears. She pushed her fingers through her damp and tousled hair.

'I'm in such a mess,' she cried.

Annie Vidler and Mabel Flowers were shocked to see their Sister in such a state. Mabel took complete control of the situation.

'Come, Sister. You are exhausted. Nurse Vidler will bring you a drink of sweet tea. Even a short sit-down will help. We won't be able to cope if you aren't well.'

Annie Vidler went to fetch some hot sweet tea and Mabel, for once forgetting her position, took Sister's cap from her head and gently combed her hair until it was neat and prim, as usual.

'There, that looks better, Sister. You had lost your cap. Now you are neat and tidy again.'

Mabel was worried, but tried not to show her feelings to Sister Mackintosh. Seeing her superior in that state had made Mabel realise that anyone, no matter who they might be, could easily succumb to stress. After all, Sister Mackintosh had worked almost non-stop around the clock on the hospital ships for weeks. Coupled with the lack of sleep was also the fact of missing meals too. Sometimes they had all been so over-stretched they would forget to eat.

Mabel Flowers sat with Sister Mackintosh until she become more like her usual self.

'I am feeling more than a little embarrassed, Nurse Mabel. Please forgive me. I am simply overwhelmed, frustrated and very, very tired.'

'We're all tired, Sister. We understand. We have to look after each other before we can look after the patients properly, don't we?'

'You are quite right, Nurse Mabel. Don't worry about me. Just a temporary lapse. I will be up and functioning quite soon. Thank you for your help and your mature understanding.'

Mabel changed the topic of conversation.

'Crispen – sorry, Sister, Chaplain Honeybourn has discovered that the soldiers and Maltese workers are building more temporary hospitals and clinics all over the island. He has heard that as many as 1,000 new nurses are being sent here from England.'

'Goodness me! I don't know where they will all sleep, but we will certainly be glad of more nurses here at this receiving centre.'

'I don't understand what is happening in the war, Sister. Do you?'

'I'm not a military expert, Mabel. It does sound as though Gallipoli has been a military disaster. I heard that all the troops have been withdrawn from the trenches. All the ones we are getting are from there. Many more have been put on hospital trains or other transport. That's all I can tell you. Of course, if we overhear military people talking, we are not supposed to listen and certainly we must not repeat what we might accidentally hear.'

'Yes, Sister. We all understand that. We can't help hearing the soldiers talking amongst themselves, though, can we?'

Everything was haphazard. Nothing was in the right place. Equipment, bedding, medicines and bandages. All had to be accounted for and kept in secure but accessible locations.

Mabel busied herself supervising yet more new nurses and completing records for Sister Mackintosh. She had temporarily pushed Chaplain Honeybourn and his Patient 355 to the back of her mind. She caught sight of Annie Vidler towards the end of her row of beds. Annie gave Mabel a wave and a tired smile. Still, Annie seemed to be coping well. She was quite undaunted by the blood and injuries before her. She didn't even raise an eyebrow at the sometimes very colourful and rich language which emanated from the patients. The following day Annie managed to catch up with Mabel and Betty Bell.

'Have you seen Sister Mackintosh today? She is in a big panic. Some of the men have developed a sickness while they have been here. Sister hopes it isn't anything contagious. She's looking for you Mabel.'

Mabel hurried to find Sister Mackintosh. She was in full

working mode, organising orderlies and soldiers as they set about erecting isolation tents.

'Ah, Nurse Flowers, there you are.' She only used Mabel's first name when they were off duty.

'I need you to equip all the nurses with face masks, at once. We may have an epidemic of something starting. We must protect the nurses or we will not be able to do our work if we fall ill.'

'Yes, Sister, I will see to it straight away.'

'Good! It seems that we might have some contaminated milk. I wonder if it is that awful tinned stuff. We aren't sure yet.'

'Best not to use that milk until we are sure, Nurse. Make sure that all water is boiled, if it's to be used for drinking.'

'Yes, Sister. I will make sure everyone is informed.'

Chaplain Honeybourn remained at the Malta hospital for the next few days. He was watching and waiting patiently for some signs of improvement in his patient's mental state. The surgeons had managed to remove most of his facial bandages. His bruised and swollen eyes were beginning to look less raw, and the new, lighter bandages would give some protection to what had been deep gashes to his head.

'Well, friend, you are looking much better now,' the Chaplain greeted him. 'I see they have managed to get you sitting in a chair. That must be more comfortable for you?'

The man still didn't speak, but gave the Chaplain a nod. He managed to show him the new plaster. He tapped on it with his knuckles.

'A couple more weeks and you might be able to walk. Yes?'

The patient held up four fingers.

'Four weeks! Is that what the doctors have told you?'

The man nodded and gave a half-smile.

Crispen Honeybourn tried to keep the conversation going, even if it was one-sided. Sooner or later he felt quite sure that his patient would say something by way of a response. Crispen was blessed with a good deal of patience and intuition. He always found the right words when he needed to.

Sometimes it was better not to talk at all. Crispen was glad that Patient 355 had been moved to the Malta hospital. It was a mile or so away from the initial casualty unit. It was away from the very awful sights and atmosphere of the receiving unit. He guessed that if the man were to stand any chance of recovery he would see it sometime soon, in a much quieter environment. Crispen Honeybourn was anxious that because he had to spend so much time with his amnesiac patient he had less time to give to other soldiers and sailors. Even in the private Malta hospital he was being called upon to perform last rites on the dying, and later more burial services, arranged in a great hurry. His great anxiety and frequent agony was having to write letters home to those parents and wives who had lost their men. As the weeks of war continued, Crispen Honeybourn found it more and more difficult to speak honestly to the men. They would ask him impossible questions. The questions kept coming and Crispen struggled to find answers which would be adequate.

'You can't believe that God would allow this to happen, Chaplain. Would you?' asked a Gallipoli soldier.

'Whose side is God on?' asked another.

Crispen felt weighed down by his own doubts and sometimes found he was lost for adequate words and he became evasive. When there was a lull in the wards and his special patient was sleeping, he thought he would allow himself the luxury of a short walk outside, away from the hospital. He wandered much further than he had intended, but he appreciated the relative peace and quiet as he walked away from the growing conglomeration of temporary military structures and the smell of hospital wards. The further he walked the fewer people and vehicles encountered. It helped his spirit to have a time of calm and a time for reflection, not to mention the fresh air. The sun sank lower in the sky and the gleaming facades became shadowy hosts of historic secrets of battles past. How he wished he was able to have his drawing pastels with him.

He knew there were many beautiful buildings in the old parts of Malta's towns. He could just glimpse in the not-too-far distance the gorgeous gold and red facades of ornate spires and domes of the churches. One day, when the war was over, he would return. He couldn't begin to guess when that might be.

As more and more soldiers had been moved on, he had been able to gather fragments of news. Of course, he told himself that sometimes the stories they told might have been somewhat embellished. They did not always ring true. He had no way of verifying all of the tales which soldiers liked to impart. It was obvious from the look of their bodies that many of the soldier's tales were feasible. Most of the soldiers Crispen had encountered so far had been from the Dardanelles, the coastal regions of Turkey. Many looked severely malnourished and very weak.

It worried Crispen Honeybourn that, even though the soldiers he had tried to help expressed their gratitude, it was not nearly enough. He felt next to useless sometimes. Maybe he should have trained to be a doctor instead of a minister of religion. He tried to banish such negative thoughts from his mind. He decided that he would think about it more seriously when he returned to England. He began talking aloud, to himself.

'I will have a great deal of thinking to do, if I ever get back to England.'

Without thinking Crispen had increased his pace and walked much further than he had intended. He became quite breathless, then a little worried that he might be lost. The atmosphere had been hot and sticky, but now he was sensing what he thought might be the south-easterly wind from the dust-laden sirocco of the Sahara. He had better stop the daydreaming and turn back to the hospital. He had an oppressive headache.

Crispen Honeybourn's mind had been on other things. He hadn't noticed the change in the weather or how far he had wandered. The darkening atmosphere soon enveloped him as he staggered on in the direction of the hospital. Suddenly, losing his balance, he stumbled over a patch of rough ground and fell onto a bush and some uneven gravel. He managed to stand up, though he had twisted his ankle and his knee was stinging. He couldn't tell if it was just grazing from the fall or whether it was an insect bite. As dusk fell quickly he knew that he had developed a temperature. It wasn't just sunstroke. Crispen thought he was nearing the hospital. He could see some shadowy figures ahead of him. He couldn't tell if they were nurses or soldiers. He feared that he might be hallucinating. There were too many figures for them to be nurses and he couldn't yet see their uniforms.

Lights around the hospital were kept low and to a minimum as technically they could still be seen by enemy forces. Guessing that he was near enough to shout for help Crispen Honeybourn waved his arms above his head and yelled as loud as he could.

'Help! Help me, someone!'

His cry was rather feeble and went unheard by the dark moving mass of bodies which were clearer to him as he staggered on towards the hospital buildings. He had another attempt.

'Help! Help me, someone!'

With just thirty yards or so to go, Crispen was defeated. He collapsed on to the gravel path leading to the Operating Department. He let out a piercing scream. This time his cries were heard. A group of Australian soldiers ran back towards him.

'Hello matey, what's the matter with you? Too much to drink?'

Crispen was unable to answer. He was totally exhausted, but he was aware that someone had come to his rescue.

'He's fainted,' said the soldier who picked him up.

'Looks like he might have got sunstroke,' the second soldier replied. 'Let's carry him to reception. Now we've got rid of our prisoners to the barracks we were going that way, weren't we?'

'He might have to wait in the queue.'

'Crikey! Look at him! This guy's a priest, chaplain or something, whatever they're called here. He's wearing a dog collar. No wonder he's feeling the heat.'

'Is he British?'

'Yes, I think so.'

'We'd better take care of him. He might have to bury us one of these days!'

The boisterous group were good-natured and made light of Crispen's predicament, who roused as he realised where he was. The Australian soldiers had improvised a stretcher and carried him in ceremonious manner ahead of the long stream of Australian and British casualties.

Sister Mackintosh and her team of nurses had by now also arrived at the Maltese hospital. She had handed over the initial receiving bay to new army and Red Cross nurses. It was a slight relief for them to be in less primitive surroundings, even if it was just temporarily.

One of the Maltese doctors gave Crispen Honeybourn a quick preliminary examination.

'He's not seriously hurt. A grazed leg, sunstroke and total exhaustion, I'd say.'

Crispen was given a sleeping draught, and, after having his leg bandaged, was carried to the less urgent ward to sleep. The doctor did thank the soldiers for their quick thinking. They went on their way.

'Poor sod! He won't know where he is when he wakes up, will he?'

'He'll think he's gone to heaven, won't he?'

'Yeah, especially when he sees those lovely nurses leaning over him in the morning.'

The conversation took on a more serious tone.

'What do you think a man like that was doing wandering about the cliff tops by himself?'

'I guess he'd be communing with nature,' one of the soldiers offered. 'Maybe he was trying to ask God to give him a reason for this bloody war!'

Sister Mackintosh encountered the Australian soldiers, without yet realising that they had brought Crispen into the hospital. She pulled herself up straight and assumed her officious, superior mode.

'Now young man,' boomed Sister Mackintosh, 'might I ask you to moderate your language? You are not on the field of battle now.'

'Sorry, Nurse.'

'It's Sister, if you please.'

'Sorry, Sister. It's just that we feel a great sense of relief having escaped the trenches, and then for us to come across a man of the cloth wandering about in the semi-darkness – well – it was very unusual to say the least. No harm was meant, Sister.'

'Very well,' Sister Mackintosh conceded.

The first man who had spotted Crispen having difficulties there in the darkness dared to ask Sister Mackintosh whether she knew the name of the man they had rescued. Until that moment she hadn't seen Crispen. All was chaos for a while, just as she had experienced at her first casualty unit. She hadn't got her own bearings, let alone managed to examine new patients.

'I don't know whether I am coming or going,' she said, in her broad Scottish accent. 'I am having to take orders from Maltese doctors as well as our military ones. It takes most of my time to keep an eye on new nurses. So, I would be very much obliged if you men would find your own unit or quarters as quickly as you can.'

Then, as an afterthought, reflecting that she must have seemed rather cross and ungrateful, she shouted after the men.

'Are any of you hurt?'

'No, Sister, we're all fair dinkum. We were in charge of a group of prisoners. Now that we've delivered them to the guard house we don't rightly know where we have to report.'

Sister Mackintosh thanked the men and directed them to a senior army officer.

'He will give you directions. Goodbye.'

Sister Mackintosh was curious. She hurried to view the ward where their rescued casualty, their 'man of the cloth', had been taken. She could hardly believe her eyes.

'It's Chaplain Honeybourn! Crispen! My goodness, what are you doing here in this dirty and dishevelled state?'

Of course, the Chaplain couldn't answer her. The sleeping draught had taken effect almost immediately. She wouldn't be able to get any explanation from him until the morning.

Sister Mackintosh's young nurses, Mabel Flowers, Annie Vidler and Betty Bell, accompanied by a dozen 'fresher' nurses, had been re-located with her. She was glad to have them. She could rely on them. The new nurses were as yet an unknown entity.

Casualties from the trenches and beach warfare were arriving daily and in greater numbers. Soldiers were having to camp out, and barrack buildings were being re-organised into hospital wards. All the private hospitals had opened their wards and deployed more of their own Maltese nurses.

'Malta is becoming the Chief Nurse of the Mediterranean,' Sister Mackintosh told the nurses proudly. Still, she felt it her duty to warn the nurses for the umpteenth time about fraternising with patients.

'We have enough problems dealing with all these sick and injured soldiers. We mustn't add to the problems by silly, immature behaviour. Do I make myself understood?'

The new younger nurses smirked behind their aprons.

'Yes, Sister,' they chorused.

'Off you go then, to your wards. I will catch up with you very shortly. Nurse Flowers and Nurse Vidler, please follow me.'

They followed Sister Mackintosh as she hurried to see their Chaplain.

'It's Chaplain Honeybourn, Sister! Just look at the state of him.'

Annie Vidler was shocked. She knelt down to feel his forehead.

'He's burning up, Sister. What has happened to him?'

'He will be all right in the morning. Apparently, he decided to take a walk by himself when things were quieter here. He must have wandered much further than he had intended. He was lost and staggering around in the semi-darkness when the Australian soldiers found him. He had fallen and gashed his knee and probably twisted his ankle too.'

'Thank goodness they found him,' said Mabel. 'I mean the Chaplain isn't a very strong type like those soldiers. He might have perished out there all night.'

'Yes,' Sister Mackintosh reflected. 'He may well have succumbed.'

Annie Vidler and Betty Bell didn't quite know what 'succumbed' meant exactly, but they guessed it wasn't good.

It was agreed that his special nurses would take it in turns during the night to keep their Chaplain cool, and quiet.

Nurse Mabel Flowers took the first watch. She couldn't take her eyes off him, except to say a prayer for him.

'Please, God, let Crispen, sorry, Chaplain Honeybourn be well again, very soon. We need him.' She paused. 'I need him, God.'

They had managed to find their Chaplain a quiet corner, though every other ward was anything but quiet. So many more troops were being brought in under darkness. More than they could cope with.

Many of the patients were quickly assessed and moved straight out again to be put on waiting hospital ships. They would be bound for Cyprus or Gibraltar and eventually for Britain.

Sister Mackintosh hadn't minded working on the hospital ships, in spite of the potential danger. She knew the routine and the clear protocols of the situation. But this – the chaos of not knowing how many patients or what kind of injuries they faced and not knowing who was actually in charge – this was very unsettling. Sister Mackintosh didn't take kindly to being ordered about by military officers as well as the Maltese doctors, both of whom frequently got in the way.

Sister Mackintosh tried her best to rally the nurses, as well as keeping her own spirits up. She was a coper, even under extreme stress, but she was an even happier coper now that Chaplain Crispen Honeybourn was under her care. She couldn't quite explain it, but Crispen Honeybourn was a very calm man in the midst of all distress. Whether it was because he was a man of God that he exuded a gentle nature she couldn't decide. He certainly bore no resemblance from the Presbyterian minister she had known since childhood in Scotland.

The nurses often overheard army officers and medical officers talking about the war. It was as though the nurses were of no real consequence, except for applying bandages to patients. They were not included in any other conversation. Sister Mackintosh, who had a good deal more knowledge than the younger nurses, often overheard quite alarming conversations, but knew she had to keep quiet about what she heard.

'Winston wants to end it all,' she heard one day. 'The generals can't agree amongst themselves. It's madness leaving it all up to a bunch of old men who can't agree.'

The officers moved away, out of Sister Mackintosh's hearing.

'One minute the naval people think it's their war and the next it's the army's responsibility. Whatever the truth of it, we seem to be losing all attempts to take the peninsula.'

Some of the Gallipoli patients, mostly from the trenches, talked openly amongst themselves about their experiences. The nurses were becoming more nervous and worried with each tale they overheard. Sister Mackintosh was mindful of Patient 355 who was mercifully asleep just then as the officers passed him by.

Nurse Mabel Flowers felt sure that Patient 355 would wake before the Chaplain and he would wonder where his companion had disappeared to. Sure enough, at the break of dawn and with the clattering sound of bedpans most of the patients were awake. Mabel was first on duty to greet the Chaplain.

'Well, good morning, Chaplain Honeybourn. You are looking much better this morning. Can I bring you some tea?'

'Oh, Mabel! Good morning to you. I feel very foolish lying here in bed alongside your patients. What a silly person I was to go off like that. I must have lost my bearings, and then the darkness came so quickly. I remember tripping over some stones, and then something sharp, like an insect bite, or a prickle of some kind. I can't believe the size of my swollen ankle.'

'Goodness, Crispen. I'll get Sister to look at it. It does look awfully red and sore.'

Mabel hurried away to find Sister Mackintosh, who was deep

in conversation with senior medical officers about which patients could be moved out to the waiting hospital ships.

It all seemed very rushed, and arbitrary. Even here, the military personnel and the doctors were arguing as to how things ought to be done.

'I'm afraid, Sister, the number of casualties has overwhelmed us. There can be no fixed order of things. We simply have to decide which patients can be saved, or otherwise, and which ones are capable of walking to the available transport.'

Sister Mackintosh was shocked that so many men were to be moved that evening, just when darkness would be upon them.

'It will be a bit fraught, Sister, but it would be very risky to move so many men in daylight.'

Mabel wanted Sister Mackintosh to look at the Chaplain's sore leg, but she was pre-occupied, not to say, flustered once again. It was another situation that she couldn't control herself.

'What is it, Nurse Flowers?'

'Sorry, Sister. I can see you have a lot to do, but could you spare a minute to look at Chaplain Honeybourn's sore leg?'

Mabel explained that the Chaplain thought he had been stung by an insect.

'I don't think it was an insect bite, Sister, but it does look very red and sore.'

'Very well, I'll come and look, Nurse. We will have such a lot to do today. We have to move many of these men out tonight. They will all require new dressings and medical supplies for their journey.'

They reached Crispen Honeybourn's bed. He was awake and sitting up, looking rather sheepish.

'I'm sorry to be such a bother, Sister. I don't quite know what I have done, but it is very sore.'

Sister Mackintosh turned to Nurse Mabel Flowers.

'What is your opinion then, Nurse?'

'The wound is too big for an insect bite, Sister. He might have fallen onto a bush or prickles of some kind. Look here, this looks like a wood splinter.'

Mabel stood back to let Sister Mackintosh examine the wound.

'Well done, Nurse Flowers. I think you may be correct. Now, we will not bother the surgeon just now. Please bring my antiseptic tray and some tweezers. We'll see if we can clean it up before it goes septic!'

'Yes, Sister, at once.'

The wound was thoroughly cleaned and medicated and, much to Nurse Mabel's relief, there was no sign of an insect bite.

'Definitely bits of twig and thorn in there, Chaplain. You'll be sore for a few days, or even a couple of weeks. At least we don't need to worry about you having malaria. Your temperature is almost back to normal. You obviously hit some sort of rocks or gravel as you fell, but the grazing is superficial.'

'I don't know what possessed me to walk all that way by myself, especially as I didn't know the terrain. I feel particularly stupid, especially as most of the chaps in here have hurt themselves in the line of duty. I need to be helping them.'

'We'll have to see if you can stand first.' Sister Mackintosh excused herself to continue her rounds with the military officers and doctors.

'Come on, Crispen,' Mabel encouraged him. 'I can use your name now Sister's gone. Hang on to my arm. We'll see if you can stand.'

He could just manage to stand, with Mabel's help.

'It's agony to walk,' he winced.

'I'll get you some pain-killers. Then I'll take you to your special Patient 355, who still has no name. He was very anxious during the night. I think he was worried that you were not there beside him. But then, all these extra casualties were brought in and he became very agitated. He totally covered himself with the blankets. He has sobbed on and off during the night.'

'Do you think he was re-living what happened to himself?'

'Very probably', replied Nurse Mabel. 'You are very observant.'

'Can he walk yet, Mabel?'

'No. He is still quite heavily plastered-up and will be for a few

53

more weeks, I guess. We have managed to get him in a wheelchair, so we will try to get him to bend his legs a little. He is obviously very limited just yet, and in pain.'

'Has he spoken at all?'

'He tried to mutter a 'thank-you' to Nurse Vidler, when she fed him.'

'Well, that's a start, isn't it?'

'Can he feed himself yet?'

Mabel Flowers was a good and conscientious nurse, but didn't wish to seem over-confident in her speculation about the patient. She was concerned about the man, who obviously had suffered some horrendous ordeal. He could barely speak and he took little interest in anything or anyone around him, except for Chaplain Crispen Honeybourn.

'I think he could feed himself, Crispen. I am not completely convinced that he wants to. He is very withdrawn. It's as if he is living with shadows.'

'Right, take me to him please, Mabel. I will see if I can get through to him.'

Patient 355 was sitting awkwardly in a wicker wheelchair. He had been moved from his bed so that one of the seriously injured soldiers could be placed there.

The man looked up and half-smiled when he recognised Crispen.

'Hello, old chap,' Crispen greeted him. He took his hand. The man's other hand was clutching the blanket tightly to his body, even though the ward was quite warm and blankets were unnecessary. Crispen guessed the blanket felt like his protection from the world. He was almost childlike in his reluctance to let the blanket drop.

'I'm sorry to have neglected you. I have hurt my leg too, so I can sympathise with you a little.'

Crispen bent down to show his bandaged leg. His handkerchief fell out of his pocket along with a few tiny globe-shaped flower heads. The man's eyes opened wide as he recognised the flowers. He pointed and struggled to say something.

'Aca— acac— acacia,' he whispered.

'What is it, chum? Say it again for me,' Crispen encouraged.

The patient repeated quite clearly, though softly, 'acacia'. For the first time since May, when he was brought from Gallipoli and into Malta on the hospital ship, the man smiled briefly through his tears. Was it the recognition of something in the man's past which had evoked a memory of something real and meaningful, or was it that he had found his voice that brought tears to his eyes? Whatever it proved to be Crispen knew that he must keep encouraging him. He was determined to keep trying.

'Fetch Sister, please, Nurse Flowers. I must tell her what we have just witnessed.'

Crispen Honeybourn had lapsed back into professional mode, addressing her as Nurse Flowers, in front of his patient.

'I'm not sure if she can come just now, Chaplain. She is with the senior officers doing the rounds. They are selecting patients who are fit enough to ship out to Gibraltar.' Mabel hurried away to see if she could locate Sister Mackintosh.

The Chaplain was impatient to try again with Patient 355.

'Did you remember the flowers from somewhere else, some other time, perhaps?'

The patient gave a slight nod. Then he frowned and shook his head, looking very confused.

'Never mind, it will come back to you. Don't worry. One day, before too long we will have you in fine shape. You have done very well for now. Just rest while I try to find Sister.'

The beds had been pushed even closer together until it was quite difficult to stand between them. The man beside Patient 355 couldn't help hearing the conversation the Chaplain had tried to encourage with his patient.

'Is he off his rocker then, Padre?'

He was taken aback by the man's tone of voice, and the language he used.

'Actually I am known as Chaplain Honeybourn, and no he isn't off his rocker as you rudely put it. He has been badly injured. He has two broken legs and is recovering from deep injuries to his face and head. He has what we call temporary amnesia due to shell shock.'

Crispen Honeybourn pleaded with the soldier to take a more understanding and sympathetic tone, should he decide to engage in conversation with his fellow patient.

'I am not sure whether you will get a better response than I have done, but I beg you to keep the conversation light and short. Will you try?' Crispen pleaded.

'I will do my best, Chaplain, sir.'

Crispen went in search of Sister Mackintosh. He hobbled through a maze of beds and frantic orderlies. Eventually he spotted Sister's entourage. They were deep in conversation with doctors and military officers. Annie, Nurse Vidler, was suddenly feeling quite important. She had been selected to follow the Medical Officer and write down all the medical details and requirements of the patients.

'I'm glad it wasn't me having to write all those big words down,' Nurse Betty Bell remarked.

'But you do know the medical words, Betty, don't you?'

'I understand most of it, but I'm not very good with the handwriting. I would be too slow trying to get it all down.'

'Well,' Annie consoled her, 'you are still doing a very important job, keeping all these folders in the correct order. I can only write in one record folder at a time. See what a pile we have already!'

All the records would have to be scrutinised by both military and medical officers before any patients could be moved.

'The Gallipoli campaign appears to have been an unmitigated disaster, Sister.'

One of the more sympathetic officers spoke quietly and probably out of turn since they were not supposed to discuss any military business with the nursing personnel.

'I'm not supposed to proffer my personal opinions, Sister, but it makes my blood boil when I know that many of these sick and injured men have had to endure over a week's treacherous sea journey in ill-equipped hospital ships to get here. You are doing a brilliant job, in the circumstances. I can see how stretched you are for space and resources. Let's see if we can get some of them at least part of the way home.'

'Thank you, sir.' Sister Mackintosh appreciated knowing that at least one officer had recognised how difficult things were.

'The Maltese have been brilliant too, sir. They are building more temporary hospital wards and clinics as fast as they can. The numbers are unprecedented and we have an extra 1,000 nurses coming from England alone.'

'It's an almost impossible task, Sister, but we must all do the best we can.'

The officer pushed the group forward.

Chaplain Honeybourn caught up with them and hobbled towards Sister Mackintosh. He beckoned her to one side.

'What is it, Crispen?' she whispered. 'Can it wait? I have to do the rounds with the officers.'

'Yes, I know, Sister. I do apologise, but I urgently need to tell you that our man 355 has spoken a few words. If there is any chance of him being taken off to Gibraltar, or even the Greek sailings, I really think he should be first in the queue. He needs a neurologist and we don't have one here.'

'Well, it isn't up to me, I'm afraid, Crispen, but if I get a chance I will speak up for him.'

'Thank you, Sister. Thank you very much. We'll speak later.'

He returned to his patient. His foot was throbbing, but he would try to find a chair – even a cardboard box would do – just something to raise his leg for a while. Crispen was determined to have another attempt to encourage the patient to speak.

'Do you mind if I put my foot up on the side of your chair?'

Crispen didn't wait for an answer. He lifted his leg and put it carefully on the edge of the wheelchair. The man, meanwhile, had manoeuvred himself back into his makeshift bed.

He had pulled the sheets and blanket close up to his neck.

He is still trying to hide, thought Crispen. He was quite sure the man was not sleeping.

'Hello again. Are you having a snooze?'

Crispen gently took one corner of the blanket to see if the man would respond.

'It's me, Chaplain Honeybourn. Sorry I wandered off. I needed to see Sister Mackintosh, but I'm back now, that is, until the doctors do their inspection. They will be here to see you very soon.'

The patient allowed Crispen to move the corner of his blanket so that he could see his face properly. His right hand was clenched tight. He was still holding a few of the yellow acacia blossom heads which had fallen from Crispen's pocket.

'I see you still have the little blossoms. What did you call them? I can't quite remember what you said they were.'

'A-c-a-c-i-a,' the man's speech faltered on every sound.

'Wonderful,' declared Crispen. 'I wouldn't have known that.'

He asked the man if he could remember where he had seen the little flowers before. The man hesitated for a moment and then shook his head. There were no more words. Perhaps they would come later.

Crispen was certain that he had triggered something in the man's brain. If only he could discover his name.

In spite of his sore leg, Crispen almost managed to stand to attention as the Senior Medical Officer appeared.

He removed his hat and offered his hand and a respectable short bow as he was introduced. Sister Mackintosh stepped back.

'Colonel, this is our Chaplain, Crispen Honeybourn. He has been our tower of strength since *HMS Goliath*.'

'Ah, yes, Honeybourn. I remember that name. Have we met before?'

'Not exactly, sir.'

Crispen was deeply embarrassed to have to admit that by some quirk of fate, and in the speed and chaos of moving hundreds of troops to different ships, he had been inadvertently directed to one of the hospital ships, and not the land troops at Gallipoli.

'Oh, I see,' said the Colonel. 'A pity, that. We were short of padres when it came to burying the dead.'

Chaplain Honeybourn, having explained himself quite adequately, was disappointed with the officer's reply. In fact, he cringed at the Colonel's cold, dismissive tone of voice. Sister Mackintosh intervened.

'Colonel, sir, the Chaplain really has been a godsend to us. He has been looking after this man who was very badly injured. He has head injuries and two broken legs. He has no memory or speech.'

Chaplain Honeybourn seized his moment.

'With respect, sir, this man needs a neurologist. His mental state is giving us great cause for concern. The doctors here have no time or, I dare say, the expertise, to deal with his problems. He really needs to be on the first ship home to England.'

'Mmm!' The Colonel played with his moustache. Then he spoke.

'What rank is he? Is he an officer?'

'I regret that we do not know that yet, sir.'

Sister Mackintosh brought the man's record folder.

'He was pulled from the sea the night *Goliath* was sunk, sir. He was almost naked and had no papers or anything with which to identify him. Hundreds were lost. The men who survived were picked up by various ships. So far none of the *Goliath*'s men knew this man.'

'So, we don't really know if this is what they are calling "shell-shock" condition or whether the man was hurt when he was flung into the sea. Has he lost his mind?'

Crispen couldn't offer a medical opinion but he was growing very impatient with the officer.

'He has lost his memory, sir?'

'It is likely to be the shock of the explosions, sir, and that many men managed to jump over the side, but hadn't judged how far out from the side they needed to jump. I have seen a number of similar cases. This one is the worst, sir.'

Sister Mackintosh pursed her lips after offering her slight understanding of the situation. She was becoming impatient with the officer too.

Suddenly, after all the hesitation and indecision, the Colonel made a decision.

'Very well, put this man on the list! The operating theatres here are overwhelmed with surgical cases. You are correct. This man needs a neurologist.'

The Colonel ordered his Captain to make the arrangements.

Patient 355 had heard every word. His body began to shake and he became more agitated than either Crispen or Sister Mackintosh had seen before. Crispen sat nearer to him and took his hands in his.

'Come now. You must try to settle. It will be the very best thing for you to get back to England where you can be helped. Do you understand what I am saying?'

The patient nodded reluctantly. There was nothing wrong with his understanding of language. He seemed just very confused and distressed when he tried to recall what had happened to him, or when he tried to remember who he was. Crispen pressed on.

'Are you afraid of being on a ship again?'

The man nodded again.

Crispen kept talking. At least if the man understood and was capable of nodding or shaking his head in response to questions, there was hope of helping him.

The Senior Medical Officer lost no time in issuing orders for Patient 355 to be placed on the first ship bound for Gibraltar, and then, hopefully to Britain, and Plymouth.

'Chaplain Honeybourn, you will accompany your patient, and I shall recommend that Sister Mackintosh be given a senior position in Gibraltar. You will take six extra nurses with you.'

The officer spoke as though the Chaplain would be in sole charge. Sister Mackintosh was taken aback at his coldness and the precision of his delivery of orders.

'Don't worry, Sister. Arrangements are all in hand. We are expecting a large group of Red Cross nurses here. They will cope admirably.'

'Well, shouldn't we stay to help them?' Nurse Mabel Flowers offered.

'These very unwell patients need you to supervise their special care on the ship to Gibraltar. You will be there in a few days, or perhaps a week. It's difficult to be precise. It all depends on how much zig-zagging the captain decides might be necessary.'

Chaplain Honeybourn didn't want to alarm the nurses unduly. He asked to speak with the officer privately.

'Sir, is it safe for any of us to travel?'

'If you mean enemy submarines… well… we can't know how many are lurking beneath the sea. We can only adopt diversionary tactics and… '

'Pray,' said the Chaplain.

The officer moved impatiently from one foot to the other, anxious to get away from awkward questions.

'That is why,' the officer continued impatiently, 'you will be placed on the Gibraltar-bound ship during the hours of darkness. My orderly will bring your papers.'

Crispen Honeybourn was not happy, but he had little reason to argue. At least it would mean that he could stay and supervise the patient who had lost his memory.

'But, Sister, I am not a doctor. I can only be useful for the man's mental condition. I'm not even sure I am qualified to do that.'

'Nonsense, Crispen, I mean Chaplain. Forgive me. I think you are probably the only person who can help this man. What will the medics do? Fill him up with drugs and put him in an asylum?'

Crispen Honeybourn was shocked.

'Surely not, Sister. He needs to find out who he is first. Then he will recover, I'm certain of it.'

Sister Mackintosh gave him a wry, sympathetic smile.

'You know, Chaplain, I think it was meant to be that you accidentally lost your place with the land forces. I heard that army padres there went out with the men into the trenches. They helped bury them by the side of the trenches, often without time to pray over them.'

'Sometimes the medical orderlies just threw bandages to the

padres and they had to help with first aid. There were so many to deal with.'

'Yes, Sister. I do know all of that. It's shocking.'

Sister Mackintosh, not wishing to brush Crispen away, asked about his sore leg.

'Let me check that for you. We can't have you going aboard the hospital ship in a poor state yourself.'

Crispen took his leg bandage off to reveal a red, pus-filled wound.

'Oh dear! We'd better get that cleaned up immediately.' Sister Mackintosh shouted for Nurse Flowers, then hurried away to make her own preparations for their move later that evening.

Nurse Mabel Flowers cleaned and disinfected Crispen's leg as gently as she could. She winced.

'You will have to get this seen to every day, Crispen. It's very sore.' She whispered his name so that Sister Mackintosh would not realise just how friendly they had become with each other.

The orderly returned.

'Here we are, sir. Your papers for the hospital ship.'

'Thank you, Orderly. How speedy and efficient of you.'

The orderly gave him a huge grin.

'Oh, there's no hanging about with the captain, sir. He'd have my guts for garters if I didn't do things right and in double-quick time.'

The orderly wished them both well.

Sister Mackintosh was annoyed at the speed of their enforced departure, but nevertheless continued to be her efficient self. She knew that nurses were being moved from one place to another all the time. She just didn't like it if she were not in control.

'Have you received your travel documents, Chaplain?'

'Yes, Sister. All present and correct. I also have papers for Patient 355. It is a shame we do not have a name for him as yet.'

'Well, that will be for the Navy to discover, won't it?'

'And you, Nurse Flowers. Have you checked with the junior nurses?'

'Yes, Sister. We are all ready to go, though not keen on being aboard a ship again.'

'Neither am I, Nurse,' admitted Sister Mackintosh, who proceeded to issue further instructions from the Chief Medical Officer.

'Apparently, we are required to be at the mess hall at 'A' barracks by 6.00 p.m. The Maltese nurses and some of the Australian soldiers and their nurses have arranged a tea party for us, followed by some light entertainment. From there we will be escorted in motor ambulances to the motor boats which will take us out to the big ship.'

'It'll be very dark, Sister. Can we take torches?'

'No, I'm afraid not. It's definitely forbidden. We have to stay very close together. The soldiers will see that we are safe.'

'What about the stretcher cases, Sister?'

'They will be carried first, hoisted up by cranes on to the big ship. There are to be no white sheets, just dark blankets. We can't give any indication to the enemy that we are moving large numbers of people.'

The nurses were alarmed that the enemy could be so close at hand.

Crispen Honeybourn took Sister Mackintosh to one side, away from patients and nurses.

'Is there a real danger, Sister?'

'I really don't know. There are always whispers about spies in our midst. Who knows? There has been talk of two missing hospital ships, but I think we should not speculate. Some ships have had to take unusual routes to fool the enemy.'

'Here we are, in the midst of it. We all have important jobs to do. It's no use making ourselves into nervous wrecks, is it, Crispen?'

Sister Mackintosh threw a glance across to Patient 355.

'Sister! I am surprised at you.'

'Sorry, Crispen. Put my rudeness down to tiredness and true frustration.'

'This man has been through a most terrible ordeal, Sister. He cannot help his condition. I have made a vow to help him. In the meantime, all any of us can do is to pray. If we can't manage that, then we just need to keep calm and try to be understanding.'

Sister Mackintosh made her excuses. She thought it better to move away before she said something she might later regret.

Crispen Honeybourn was not going to let Sister Mackintosh disappear after that. If things were to move smoothly and swiftly he might not be able to enlist her help for his patient. The medical officers had certainly moved with great speed and decisiveness through the many dozens of casualties who needed to be moved.

Casualties from the trenches were being brought in constantly. The wards were overflowing into outside sheds, the barracks and even church halls.

'Sister, please wait. I appreciate how dreadfully busy you all are, but please see that it is imperative that we have some kind of sedative for Patient 355? I can't see him being hoisted up by the crane, without him screaming with fear. Can you trust me with the medication? Or would it be better if Nurse Flowers were to take it?'

Sister Mackintosh considered Crispen's dilemma.

'I will let you take it. Nurse Flowers will have more than enough to do. I do concede that Patient 355 is an exceptional case. I do most sincerely apologise if I seemed tactless.'

'Thank you, Sister. It is the only solution if we don't want a further nightmare-scenario.'

Crispen Honeybourn was quite certain that his patient knew what was happening, even if he couldn't talk. He would try to keep a conversation going and give the man one piece of information at a time. There would be no point in telling him everything at once. The man's thoughts were jumbled enough.

The nurses had washed and dressed the man in warm, loose-fitting clothes, suitable for his onward journey after the barracks tea party.

'Here he is, Chaplain. Clean and tidy for you. We have even given his long hair a trim.'

'Thank you both, Nurse Mabel and Nurse Annie. Let me shake your hands. We might all be separated after the tea. We are being moved out in small groups and in semi-darkness as the entertainment begins.'

'I hope we get to see some of the entertainment,' Annie said. 'It'll be the only fun part of this awful place, won't it?'

Mabel scoffed.

'You mean fraternising with the Australian soldiers, don't you?'

'Of course! They're so sun-bronzed and handsome, aren't they?'

Annie giggled.

'Does that mean you think our soldiers are not sun-bronzed and handsome?' Mabel teased.

'Well, put it this way, you can't help noticing the difference!'

Crispen Honeybourn smiled to himself as he overheard the nurses chattering and giggling together. It lent a more casual air to their very difficult work.

'Our boys look so pale and skinny by comparison,' said Annie.

Their Chaplain smiled and then assumed his professional role.

'Excuse me, ladies. I need to go now and finish off some letters home for some of my other charges.'

Letters home were the saddest part of the Chaplain's work. He had to break the news of their son's death in action, or their injured men who couldn't write for themselves. He was sometimes writing to young wives who may or may not have children to care for. Crispen's heart went out to them all. He sometimes spent hours over his letters. Each one was very individual. He didn't write the same words to everyone. He did his very best to write a personal and caring message. He could visualise all their faces as they received their letters.

Crispen Honeybourn sat beside his Patient 355, who watched intently as he sealed each envelope carefully. The final one completed, he heaved a sigh of relief.

'Sometimes it is a most heart-rending job,' he told his patient.

He held the envelopes up for his patient to see.

'This one is to Essex, this one to London, and these two are going to Yorkshire and Grantham in Lincolnshire.'

Crispen deliberately read out the destination names. He hoped that perhaps one day the man might show some sign of recognition. Patient 355 was recovering physically, and once the face bandages had been partially removed he was taking more interest in his surroundings, once he could actually turn his head. He didn't quite understand the frantic hurrying to and fro of the nurses, but he had realised that a larger than usual group of officers had something to do with it.

Chaplain Honeybourn took his letters to the post orderly, who would ensure that they were sent in the next available mailbag destined for England.

'God only knows when they will get there,' he pondered. He couldn't even tell if the post would be going via a land route or by the next possible sea route. Either way the letters will have travelled many miles before the sad news would reach their recipients.

Once the decision to move suitable patients during darkness had been taken, everything in the wards and surrounding buildings began to move at a much quicker pace. Blankets and waterproof garments and sheets were taken to the motor ambulances, and emergency equipment was quickly counted, logged, and boxed-up ready for use on the hospital ship.

Nurses Mabel Flowers and Annie Vidler collected waterproof garments for their wheelchair patients.

'They don't realise it yet,' Mabel whispered to Annie Vidler. 'They will have to be hoisted up onto the big ship by crane. They'll get soaking wet more than likely.'

'How are we going to get them dressed if they're going to the tea party first?'

'We'll have to get their trousers on now. They can sit on their jackets until it is time to move them.'

Three new Red Cross nurses appeared along with Nurse Betty Bell and several orderlies to help dress the wheelchair patients for their arduous journey later.

Sister Mackintosh anxiously surveyed the scene.

'Where is Chaplain Honeybourn? We could do with him here now.'

'I think he has taken his post to the clerk, Sister. He will be here soon. He is designated to look after Patient 355.'

'Yes, I know that Nurse Bell,' Sister said impatiently. 'I need to give him this sedative for his patient, without the Medical Officer noticing.'

Sister Mackintosh turned towards her senior nurse Mabel Flowers.

'We can't have another hysterical incident when they hoist the man from the motor boat to the ship, can we?'

Mabel realised then that Sister Mackintosh did indeed have another less patient side to her character. When Mabel had been newly qualified she had been very aware that she herself was under scrutiny and had to get everything right. Now that she had become more confident in her own abilities she was able to take a look at those around her and begin to recognise qualities in other people, without necessarily being judgmental.

She guessed that was what her parents had described as maturity. *Anyhow,* thought Mabel, *Sister was strict but helpful with me in the beginning.*

'If you don't know how to proceed,' Sister Mackintosh had stressed, 'you come and ask.'

Sister Mackintosh was waiting for the Chaplain.

The Chaplain returned from his mailing mission.

'You are still limping, Chaplain Honeybourn. How are you going to manage?' Sister Mackintosh asked.

'Well, I found a makeshift walking stick.' He waved a broom handle in the air.

'Look, if we cut a few inches off it will help steady me. Don't worry, Sister. I shall have two orderlies with me. The leg is a bit sore but the M.O. said it was a superficial wound and it will heal before long.'

Sister Mackintosh passed the sedative tablets to him.

'Please do not let the M.O. see that I have given them to you. I am expected to administer them myself, but I shall be elsewhere when your patient needs to take them.'

'You can trust me implicitly, Sister. Give me the instructions.'

'Very well. He must have two of these tablets half an hour before he is to be lifted on to the hoist. He will be flaked out. He will not know anything about the moving until well after he wakes up in his berth – or will he be placed in a cot? I'm not sure. I hope he isn't placed near a lot of rowdy Australians.'

The Chaplain smiled at Sister's turn of phrase.

'Well, I expect after the tea and the entertainment there will be quite a few rowdy bits of singing at least. What do you say, Sister?'

'I am sure it will engender much mirth and silly behaviour!'

Sister Mackintosh thanked him.

'Thank you, Chaplain, Crispen. I don't expect I will see you again until we are all in place on the new hospital ship.'

'It'll be déjà-vu, won't it, Sister? Except this time, I will have a proper role and I shan't be there by some accident.'

'Yes, it will, Crispen. I am relieved that you didn't end up in the trenches. There have been such stories of army padres having to take shovels and bury the dead themselves by the side of the trenches and with little time for prayers. The conditions have been appalling. There were the rotting corpses of dead horses as well as soldiers. Many died in the trenches while they were also suffering malaria or dysentery.'

Sister Mackintosh became quite emotional having to relate all of those unpleasant facts to Crispen. She wiped her face with her handkerchief.

'Well, we are all glad that you are here. You have been really wonderful with this poor man. Enjoy your tea and the entertainment. I will find you on the ship eventually. I hope we will be on our way to Southampton, or it might be Plymouth. We will have to wait and see.'

They looked at each other thoughtfully.

'Would you like me to say prayers now, before we go, Sister?'

'You are welcome to try, Chaplain,' she said, reverting to his proper mode of address. She took leave of him and began assembling groups of orderlies, nurses and clerks ready for the barracks festivities. As soon as they had organised the groups of patients and they had vacated their beds, another influx of injured men took their place together with yet another group of volunteer nurses from the Malta Red Cross.

Chaplain Honeybourn managed to gather a small group of soldiers, sailors and nurses, who thought that maybe a few prayers and a blessing would be the only positive thing they could do. Then they were on their way to the barracks mess hall.

The Australian soldiers had made the mess hall look like a theatre.

'Look!' squealed Annie Vidler, with sheer delight. 'Look what they have done to the place. There's fancy curtains, candles on the tables and boxes for us to sit on. It's just like the music hall back in Shoreditch.'

None of Annie's nurse friends had ever been to a music hall, though they had heard about a rather saucy singer called Marie Lloyd.

The makeshift box tables had been covered in white paper for a dainty tablecloth, and somehow they had managed to find tin plates. It wouldn't have to matter that they weren't fine bone china.

The soldiers had been alerted that their audience, such as it was, would disappear a few at a time. It had all been cleverly planned. The darkened rear of the hall near to the exit doors was heavily shrouded with blackout drapes, arranged carefully over some scaffolding and wide stepladders. That would allow for wheelchairs to pass through. Two orderlies would man the gap in the draped curtains, and as each group of patients were brought through they would open and close the drapes as quickly and quietly as they could between each timed musical item.

Sandwiches, cake and apples were served as the entertainment began.

Some of the Australian soldiers opened the programme with a

very boisterous rendition of 'Waltzing Matilda', which seemed to have dozens of verses. The audience were encouraged to join in when it got to the chorus.

'It don't matter if you don't know the words, folks, just give it all you've got with 'la la-la la la!''

So the steady evacuation of patients and nurses began. Some managed to grab their party food as they left. The soldiers carried on with the show, regardless of the discreet activity elsewhere in the hall.

'Now then, ladies and gentlemen, one of our Irish chaps is going to play the spoons. You can help him along with the song if you like, or whistle the tune if you don't know the words.'

A very loud rendition of 'It's a Long Way to Tipperary' followed. The audience happily whistled or clapped their way through the song.

'Well done, everybody,' shouted the compère. 'Now, after all that noise, we have a real treat for you. Miss Santini, one of our lovely Maltese nurses, is going to play a beautiful calm piece on the violin. It's called 'Chanson de Matin' and is by Mr. Edward Elgar. Please give a warm welcome to Miss Maria Santini and her accompanist Mr. d'Souza.'

The audience listened intently, the 'escapees' hardly daring to move until the piece ended to rapturous applause. The compère was ecstatic in his praise of the music.

'Well, I have never heard anything so beautiful. I know that the whole audience really appreciated it. If nothing else, you all put your glasses down.'

More rapturous applause followed, allowing another group of patients and their nurses to make their exit as swiftly as they could. The compère spoke again.

'I am pleased to announce our second classical item before we launch into our communal sing-song. Please welcome a gentleman tenor, Mr Bruno Fontana. He is going to sing a piece by George Frederick Handel. It is called 'Silent Worship'.

Mary Wilson was spellbound and Annie Vidler couldn't take

her eyes off Patient 355. She nudged the Chaplain to listen to his patient.

> *'Did you not hear my lady go down the garden singing,*
> *Blackbird and thrush were silent*
> *To hear the alleys ringing… '*

Patient 355 was gently humming along – now and then he seemed to be remembering some of the words towards the end of each phrase. Chaplain Honeybourn couldn't quite believe what he was hearing. There were tears trickling down the man's face.

'Did you recognise the music?'

The man turned and whispered.

'Is it Charlie?'

'No,' Crispen answered. 'The singer's name is Bruno Fontana. I believe he sings in the cathedral here.'

Sister Mackintosh had been keeping a close eye on the two of them.

'It's good that your patient is beginning to regain some memory, Crispen. It would help if he could remember who Charlie was. That is twice we have heard Charlie's name. At least it is something to go at, isn't it?'

'I'll keep trying, Sister.'

Sister Mackintosh had been anticipating a different kind of upset, but she thought it prudent to ignore what had just occurred and get the patient and the Chaplain out as quickly and gently as she could.

'Come on, Chaplain Honeybourn. It's your turn to go in the motor ambulance. Nurse Flowers and Nurse Vidler will accompany you both.'

'What about you, Sister?'

'I shall follow you shortly, with the last of our group. I shall have Nurse Bell and four of the Red Cross nurses with me. I will see you on the big ship.'

'Should I give the patient his sedative now, Sister?'

'Yes, that's a good idea. Here have the last few sips of my tea.'

They both watched Patient 355 swallow his pills with the tea. The orderly came to help transfer him to a stretcher and out, through the dark curtains and into the night, and then to the safety of the ambulance.

Sister Mackintosh waved them off and returned to the tea party until it was her turn to move with the final group.

Crispen Honeybourn breathed a sigh of relief. His patient was soon asleep and totally unaware of being moved from ambulance to small boat and then via the hoist onto the big ship waiting in the harbour.

Nurse Mabel Flowers felt she could breathe more easily once they were away from Sister Mackintosh.

'Crispen, we heard the patient humming. Wasn't it wonderful?'

'Do you mean that it was a beautiful song, or wonderful that he was able to hum along with the tune?'

'Well, both really. It was wonderful, too, that the soldiers were able to put on the entertainment and tea for us.'

Crispen agreed. He was thinking hard. Clearly his patient knew the song very well, but from where? Had he been a chorister? He was intrigued to know who Charlie was. Somewhere in the man's past Charlie had been of great importance to him. For his memory to be so jogged was a promising sign.

'I think this young man is getting flashbacks of recognition. It seems a small incident but I think it will prove to be the beginning of him regaining more pieces of his life's journey, terrible though it has been for him.'

Mabel was immensely proud to know Crispen. He had such a huge heart, such compassion, understanding and patience.

'I am sure you will be the person to help him, Crispen.'

'Well, I do hope so Mabel, but you know it is quite possible that we may be separated when we reach Britain. Our patient will certainly have to be hospitalised somewhere. God knows where.'

'Do you think that God really does know where, Crispen?'

'We will have to pray for help,' he answered.

Mabel thought that was a strange, enigmatic answer. Could it be that the Chaplain was beginning to doubt? Only time would tell.

Both of them had much to occupy their inner thoughts that dark, frightening night. Mabel pondered her own future. Would she be a nurse for the rest of her life? Or dare she even contemplate finding a good husband and raise a family. It seemed ridiculous to contemplate that when the world was in chaos.

Crispen Honeybourn was toying with the idea of asking permission to take a sabbatical. He could still offer his services to sick and injured people, whether they were soldiers, sailors or among the home civilian population. He needed time to think about God and religion. Perhaps he should take time to think about some kind of career change.

Annie Vidler wished they could have stayed longer at the tea party. It had been the most fun she had experienced for years. It had been good to suspend reality, even for a short time.

'I wonder what we missed at the concert?'

Annie had joined Mabel and Crispen, interrupting their quiet conversation. Both Mabel and Crispen remembered.

'Yes,' said Crispen cheerily, glad of a diversion.

'They were to have a communal sing-song, led by a Harry Lauder impersonator. I think they were to have songs from Australia, Ireland and Scottish repertoire. I would have enjoyed that.'

'We all would,' laughed Annie.'

They would all hear later how the Harry Lauder sound-alike had succeeded in making Sister Mackintosh's day even more special.

'Ladies and gentlemen,' the compère had announced with great aplomb. 'I have it on very good authority that in our midst we are most blessed to have a Scottish Sister Mackintosh.'

The compère looked first towards the Medical Officer, and then directly towards Sister Mackintosh, who was then blushing.

'Sister Mackintosh has been a brilliant godsend training new nurses to look after you lot. So this next item, which begins our sing-song is dedicated especially to Sister Mackintosh.'

The compère introduced the Harry Lauder sound-alike who sang directly to Sister Mackintosh before inviting the audience to sing the words of the chorus.

'I love a lassie, a bonnie, bonnie lassie
She's as pure as the Lily in the dell
She's as sweet as the heather, the bonnie
purple heather
Mary ma scotch blue bell'

Buoyed by the audience response, the singer carried on. There were obviously a lot of Scots soldiers in the audience. They sang with great gusto.

'I love a lassie, a bonnie, bonnie lassie,
If you saw her you would fancy her as well
I met her in September, popped the question in November
So soon I'll hae 'er to myself.
Her faither has consented, so I'm feeling quite contented
Cause I've been and sealed the bargain in a kiss.
I sit and weary, weary, when I think about my dearie
And you'll always hear me singing this...'

The Harry Lauder Collection

'Come on, join in, – *I love a lassie*...' the singing went on and on. One of the soldiers even persuaded Sister Mackintosh to take a turn with him around the floor until she became quite breathless.

After all the jollity and away from the barracks, the night was misty and muggy, as the last of the Malta patients were safely aboard the hospital ship which had been waiting for them, anchored out of Valletta harbour. There had been a lengthy departure due to a French ship being unprepared in time to make their hasty journey away from Malta. Rumours were circulating that both ships were having to take devious zig-zag routes in order to confuse any enemy submarines lurking in the waters below.

Almost all the crew and the passengers – patient or nurse – were living in a high state of anxiety, wondering whether they would ever get to Britain. Patient 355 was still heavily drugged at the start of their homeward journey, but sooner or later he would wake to realise that all his earlier fears might be compounded.

The nurses tried their best to remain cheerful. In fact, they didn't have too much time to think of what might happen. Yet again they all had to adapt to new surroundings and new ways of dealing with patients. Some of the patients who had, of necessity, been drugged, had been very heavy to carry, and orderlies were now needing help to ease their strained backs.

Part Three

'Well, at least we know there won't be hundreds more joining us, Mabel.'

'That's true, Annie, though I am not entirely sure whether some of these patients will be taken off at Gibraltar.'

Sister Mackintosh was none the wiser. She was annoyed at the code system which the new Medical Officer had imposed on them. Nurse Bell said she would never remember them all. She became very flustered.

'S-I Slightly injured; B-D Badly Injured; N-H No hope; N-O Needs an operation; M-U Mentally unstable.'

Betty kept repeating the list.

'I've forgotten F-B-C, Annie.'

'That's Frequent Bandage Changes.'

Sister Mackintosh re-assured the nurses.

'Don't worry. We will continue with my usual rounds. We will read the records of each one as we go through the ranks.'

'That's another thing, Sister,' Annie Vidler spoke out.

'We have to separate the officers from the other ranks and we have to call the officers by their titles. It's all too much to remember.'

Sister Mackintosh could see that there would be a few clashes of opinion on this part of the journey home. She urged the nurses to remain calm. If they became anxious about anything, they were to report back to her. She would deal with any awkward situations.

Chaplain Honeybourn was working his way through the ship after making sure that Patient 355 was comfortable. He was very relieved that the morphine tablets had taken effect. Almost twenty-four hours later the patient was still sleepy and unaware of how he had been strapped to a stretcher and hoisted on to the ship. He had been placed in a quiet bed, quieter than the Malta hospital.

The Chaplain hobbled along with the help of his improvised walking stick. He was familiarising himself with any new faces and re-assuring the patients he recognised along the way. It was a long ship and would take some time to walk the length of it. Sister Mackintosh spotted him with his notebook. He was trying to bend down to speak with a new patient.

'Chaplain Honeybourn. Should you be kneeling like that? How is your injured ankle?' she asked.

'Hello, Sister. I'm fine, truly. It's still a bit sore, but not as sore as some of these chaps. It'll be fine in a few days. All we need is a smooth journey home and some sunshine.'

Sister Mackintosh agreed. She watched him put his notebook back in his pocket.

'I'm intrigued, Chaplain. What exactly do you find to write in your notebook?'

The Chaplain hesitated and scratched his head as he thought of an appropriate answer to Sister's question.

'Well, I write the date and time and each man's name, home address and religion. That is, if they want to give it to me. Then I ask about their injuries and how they are feeling at that moment. I ask if I can do anything for them.'

'Do you remember them, Chaplain?'

'Of course, Sister. You would be surprised at the things they tell me. All in confidence, you understand.' Sister Mackintosh nodded.

'I hear about their home, their families, their special interests, and, of course, they talk about their hopes and fears. This is what I remember about them.'

Sister Mackintosh was full of admiration for the Chaplain. He was always calm and understanding. He never seemed to show anger or annoyance, even with soldiers who could sometimes be rude and offensive to his position.

Just for once Sister Mackintosh let formality, in public, slip on that occasion.

'Crispen Honeybourn. You are a wonderful man, a strength-giver. I wish that I could be more like you.' Sister Mackintosh left him to study his precious notebook.

Several days later, when they had sailed a good number of miles through the Mediterranean and towards the Atlantic Ocean, Sister Mackintosh found the Chaplain again. By this time the Chaplain had also discovered the crass coding system of patients.

'I have taken issue with the Medical Officer about the appalling way he has issued these orders, Sister.'

'Good for you, Crispen,' she whispered, so that no one would hear.

'Am I allowed to know what the Medical Officer's response was?'

'I am afraid I was coldly informed that it was not my domain.'

'However, I tried very diplomatically to point out that seeing N-H – signifying 'No Hope' – was not helpful for the other patients to see. I was calmly informed that the N-H patients would receive morphine and no further treatment, until eventually, they would become my domain.'

Sister Mackintosh had never seen the Chaplain so crestfallen. She brushed protocol aside and linked arms with him.

'Come on, Crispen. We'll have a nightcap. I think I saw some cocoa in my new cupboard.'

Sister Mackintosh was determined that she would tackle the Medical Officer the next morning. In the meantime, she and her Chaplain sipped cocoa and nibbled shortbread biscuits. They talked through much of the night.

The quietness of the ship's personnel and patients meant they were more relaxed. The cocoa helped. The ease of friendship meant that Sister Mackintosh chattered more openly about herself than she had ever felt the desire to do before. So, when Crispen Honeybourn asked whether she had plans for their arrival home in England, she smiled a smile that he hadn't seen before.

'Well, I'm actually a Scottish lassie, from Glasgow.'

She remembered the soldier singing for her at the Malta tea

party. It made her laugh out loud when she thought of it. Crispen laughed too.

'Seriously, Crispen. I don't really know. There will be a huge need for nurses all over the country. I have no idea whether I still have a family in Glasgow and they have no idea about me. Perhaps I should go and find out. We haven't seen each other for many years.'

'How very sad,' Crispen offered.

Crispen Honeybourn was even less certain about his own future. He had always thought that his devotion to God and the church would be the entire purpose of his life. Now he wasn't so sure. He wasn't sure if he should be talking about his own life. He had been brought up to serve others. The personal life was of secondary importance.

'I really want to help our post-shock amnesiac patient, Sister. I don't know yet how I will manage it, but I desperately want to try. I really fear for him if he has no one to stand by him.'

'Surely you can't be responsible for him, Crispen? I imagine that he will be sent to a mental hospital, won't he? There are thousands of patients like him in military hospitals.'

'That's just it. Many of those patients have suffered what is called shell shock and they have many different kinds of mental problems. Some will have lost their minds completely. This patient still has his intellect. What he has lost is his memory of a horrific accident. He had a bad gash to his head, but that is healing, along with his legs. He needs help to recover the memories of that dreadful night, and when he does he will be able to come out of the shadows that he is living with just now. It will be painful for him, but when he can remember who he is he will be able to go forward again.'

Sister Mackintosh listened intently.

'Crispen, won't he be able to get that help in hospital?'

Crispen could hardly bear to relate some of the awful things he had witnessed. Before he could bring himself to speak, he asked Sister Mackintosh if she really wanted him to describe what he had seen.

'I'm a tough woman, Crispen. This war has opened my eyes to many horrors that mankind has inflicted upon itself.'

He told how some men in the field of battle experiencing constant shelling became hysterical and deeply shocked. Often, when they tried to run for safety they were shot as deserters. They were sometimes called cowards or traitors.

Sister Mackintosh nodded. She spoke softly so that the young nurses would not overhear their conversation.

'So I have heard,' she whispered.

'Sister, I do fear that the doctors in the field hospitals are really overwhelmed. There are so many physical injuries to deal with and very little in the way of operating equipment. It really points to the fact that, awful though it is, the mentally depressed or shocked men are often drugged just to keep them quiet until they can be moved on.'

'Is that what will happen to Patient 355?' she asked.

'I don't know yet, Sister. He may need surgery to his face. I would say that he is actually quite fortunate to be on this ship and we are almost home. He is sure to be placed in a surgical unit somewhere.'

The two other nurses joined them and shivered as they heard the conversation.

Sister Mackintosh and the Chaplain were not able to speak in confidence about their patients. The younger nurses were now hovering, Chaplain Honeybourn lightened the conversation as they each asked the others what they would do when they arrived back in England.

'What about you, Crispen? Do you have a family somewhere who will be worrying about you?'

'No, I'm afraid there is no one I can tell you about.'

Crispen looked unusually pensive.

'You see,' he faltered.

'Both my parents died when I was only a few months old. It was an epidemic of Spanish influenza. My father had been an Anglican assistant vicar with a small London parish.'

'Were you placed with relatives then?' Sister Mackintosh asked.

'No. The bishop and the Board of Guardians took the decision to place me in an orphanage for sons of the clergy.'

Sister Mackintosh was astounded and the other nurses were speechless. They wanted to ask more about his childhood, but Sister Mackintosh sent them on various errands to avoid embarrassing Crispen any further.

'Well, Crispen, you obviously had a very good education. Was it very harsh? It must have been very difficult for you without parents.'

'On the contrary. I think I was extremely lucky. I wasn't the only orphan and it wasn't particularly harsh. It was all quite orderly and disciplined. I loved learning. You see, I had been fostered out to a family until I was deemed old enough to be sent to theological college.'

'Was that your own choice, Crispen?'

'I can't rightly remember, Sister. I think it was assumed to be a natural progression, following in my father's footsteps.'

The further the hospital ship sailed through the Strait of Gibraltar and then on through the Atlantic, the more optimistic her passengers allowed themselves to feel. The nurses mostly dreamed of home and how much they would enjoy having their own bath, before they dreamed of family, or even the sweethearts they once had. Many of their sweethearts would have been lost in the war somewhere.

'I'll never feel clean again,' said Nurse Annie Vidler. They all agreed that they had very much missed the comforts of home.

The medical officers were anxious that their records would all be seen in the best light. They pondered what their next posting and position might be when they returned to England. Everyone, from the Chief Medical Officer down to the lowliest orderly was worrying where they would be sent next. Many of the sailors hoped they would stay in Southampton, at least for a while. Some just contemplated a quieter life and hoped to find the families they had left behind. There were a great many mixed emotions as everyone anticipated their futures. Joyful anticipation sometimes gave way to feelings of uncertainty and worry.

The nurses wondered whether they would still be together.

'Clearly, we can't all be sent to the same hospitals. I wonder who decides?' Nurse Mabel Flowers questioned. Even Sister Mackintosh couldn't give her an answer.

Life would certainly be very different, especially for those who had been away for a long time. Some soldiers, sailors and nurses had been away for three or more years, with no possibility of home leave. Everything would be different. Those who had not managed to keep in touch with families wondered whether they might even be able to find them again.

'I wonder how much of London has been bombed?' asked Annie Vidler.

Everyone quietened down, in order to think. The nearer they sailed towards Southampton the mood swung between excitement to anxiety and back again.

Chaplain Honeybourn, in his official capacity was still having to say prayers over dying patients, who hadn't quite made it home. He was still having to write letters on behalf of patients and, incredibly, still arranged evening prayers on board ship, for those who wished to be present in the tiny ship's chapel. He was concerned about Patient 355. He wasn't able to walk unaided just yet. Crispen Honeybourn tried to keep the man occupied. Crispen wasn't sure how much the man realised about the journey home and about the tricky manoeuvre of disembarking the ship. He had little in the way of spontaneous speech, but he certainly understood Crispen when he spoke with him. The man would nod in response. He would say 'thank you' to nurses, and to Crispen.

'Shall we try some more drawing today?' Crispen would ask.

'Thank you,' the man nodded.

'Here, we'll share my pastels. You are getting too good with the pencil. I'll show you how to shade things.'

They sat together in a quiet corner of the saloon on the mess deck, the Chaplain's box of pastels placed on a small table between them. He showed his patient how to hold the crayons and gently work at a scene of differently coloured trees. A different shade of green every time.

'If I didn't know better,' Crispen said quietly, 'I could swear that you have done this before. You seem to have a natural gift for line and perspective.'

The man didn't answer. He was totally absorbed. Crispen noticed that the man naturally measured things with his thumb, like a true artist. Whatever he was drawing he seemed very concerned that he balanced his subjects with perfect symmetry. If he was not satisfied with his effort he very swiftly managed to erase it with a cloth. There were no smudges.

The man's mental state was still very confused, but he seemed less tense. His facial features were less contorted when strangers passed him by. He hadn't made any effort to speak voluntarily to strangers.

Sister Mackintosh stopped by to bring them cold drinks. She peered over the patient's drawing with admiration.

'Well done!' she exclaimed. 'I really like that. I am glad to see that you are coming out of your shell at last.'

The patient didn't speak but gave Sister Mackintosh a small nod. Crispen signalled her to move on. He knew that any prolonged conversation would result in the man becoming agitated. His hands would shake and then his head would jerk up and down until all became quiet again. Crispen excused himself.

'I just want to have a word with Sister Mackintosh. You will be all right by yourself for a few minutes, won't you?'

The man nodded and Crispen thought he detected a very slight smile.'

Crispen followed Sister Mackintosh.

'Sorry, Sister. I had to usher you along like that. I didn't mean to sound rude.'

'That's all right. Was there a problem, Crispen?'

'I am learning each day how Patient 355 responds to his immediate surroundings. He is still, obviously, in deep shock and he develops tremors of the hands and head when he feels mentally challenged.

'I have experienced this condition many times, Crispen. It could take years for him to fully recover. Perhaps he never will. Let's hope he finds a good doctor. They aren't all sympathetic, you know.'

Crispen Honeybourn hurried back to his patient to discover him in an agitated state. He had spilt some water on his beautiful sketches.

'It wasn't our fault, Chaplain. We only wanted to see his drawing. Then he got upset with us.'

Nurse Mary Wilson and one of the new Red Cross nurses from Malta had stopped to talk with the patient.

'He feels crowded,' Chaplain Honeybourn explained gently. 'It's like a sort of claustrophobia. He cannot cope with groups of people, just yet.'

'There's only two of us,' Nurse Wilson offered. 'We weren't making a noise or anything.'

'Well, thank you both.' Crispen calmed the situation and the nurses left them alone. They were obviously feeling rebuffed and they walked rather haughtily to the outer deck.

They had not noticed the man walking nonchalantly behind them. The hot afternoon sun had begun to disappear and there was a slight chill in the air as the skies darkened. Nurse Mary Wilson shivered.

'Ooh! I wish I'd put my cape on now. Come on, let's go below,' she urged her Maltese friend.

The man caught up with them.

'Here, lovely lady. Have my jacket.'

He placed his jacket around Mary's shoulders.

'Well I never,' she giggled.

'Thank you, kind sir.'

As Mary and her friend turned to face the man, Mary realised that he was Bruno Fontana, the singer from the tea party.

'What might you be doing on a military ship?' Mary asked.

'Well, it's a long story, lovely Sheila.'

His blue eyes twinkled as he continued to tease her.

'Come and meet me for a drink this evening and I'll tell you my life story if you like?'

The Maltese nurse was embarrassed and said they should move on before they were caught fraternising. Sister Mackintosh would not be pleased.

'My name is Mary, not Sheila,' Mary pouted.

'And his name is not Bruno Fontana,' the Maltese nurse whispered in Mary's ear.

'How do you know?'

'Because his accent is Australian. He's not Maltese or British.'

'Go on, you're joking!' Mary turned to the man.

'Are you Australian?' she asked him.

'I'm a man of the world, pretty one,' he said, laughing.

They had sauntered along the entire length of the deck before the man relieved Mary of his jacket. The two nurses ran off, hoping that Sister Mackintosh had not spotted them.

Annie Vidler had observed the threesome as they were strolling along, laughing and joking together.

'What on earth were you thinking of?' Annie demanded.

'Keep your hair on. You sound just like Sister Mackintosh.'

'We was only talking.'

'Flirting, more like. If Sister catches you she will be furious, I can promise you that.'

'Well,' said Mary crossly. 'If he's Australian and not even a soldier, what's he doing on a troop ship going back to England?'

Annie considered her answer.

'And anyway, why has he got a foreign name?' Mary added.

'I don't know, Mary, but I will find out.'

The Maltese nurse was looking nervously around. This was her first posting as a Red Cross nurse and she did not wish to jeopardise her future career.

'I will see you later at supper, Mary.'

Mary Wilson waved her friend goodbye, then feigned a sulky expression.

'Stop it, Mary! Don't be so childish,' Annie scolded her. 'Don't you realise that your silly behaviour is why you were sent to Lesbos. It seems you haven't learned anything.'

'Well, Annie Vidler. I remember when you were reprimanded for silly behaviour.'

'Well, I've grown up a bit since then.'

Annie Vidler left Mary to ponder her situation. She wanted to discuss the whole incident with Chaplain Honeybourn before anything got to Sister Mackintosh. He was the soul of discretion and might know what Bruno Fontana was doing there. It seemed that the man had managed to roam around the ship unaccompanied and unchallenged. No one seemed to know what he was doing there. He had gone unchecked for some time.

By the time Annie had located the Chaplain it was evening. She had missed supper, not that she felt like eating anything. The lights on the ship had been dimmed and patients were trying to sleep. If they couldn't get to sleep they pretended, so as not to upset anyone else.

Finally, Nurse Annie Vidler managed to locate the Chaplain. He was in a tiny side room, off the saloon. It was always quiet there and he could work at his papers, undisturbed.

She crept into the side room and apologised for disturbing him.

'Chaplain, is it all right if I come and have a word with you?'

'Yes, of course, Nurse Vidler. Do come in and sit down.'

She closed the sliding door behind her so that nobody could hear what she had to say to the Chaplain in private.

'May I call you Crispen now, Chaplain?'

'Yes, of course, Annie. What can I do for you?'

'Well, Crispen, do you remember the singer Bruno Fontana from the Malta tea party?'

'Yes, of course I do. What a character he was.'

'Well, he's here on the ship. He's been flirting with some of the nurses. At least I know of two of them. And guess what?'

Annie paused for breath. She felt like a schoolgirl who was

telling tales. Still, she did feel that something was not right and Crispen Honeybourn was the only person she could confide in and hope he wouldn't chide her for doing so.

'I am intrigued. Go on.'

'Well, his accent is not Maltese at all. He's Australian. His clothes are not those of a soldier or sailor. He's certainly not a doctor or even a medical orderly. I would know if he was. So, who is he and why is he here on the hospital ship?'

Crispen listened without making any comment. He had already formed his own opinion of the man, though he really had no concrete reasons for thinking him a devious character. He certainly wouldn't want to spread ill-informed rumours.

'I am sure there will be an explanation, Annie. Don't you worry about it. I will find out if I possibly can.'

Crispen steered the conversation to other things.

'By the way. I seem to have lost track of Nurse Mabel Flowers and Nurse Betty Bell.'

'Yes, so have I, Crispen. This is a much bigger ship than you think and I find it is easy to get lost when we are away from the hospital wards.'

'I expect by the time we have memorised all the corridors and ward decks we will be home,' Crispen said in a spirit of cheerfulness.

'Not long now, Annie. What will you do when we are home?'

Annie didn't have time to answer him. Sister Mackintosh, who knew her way around very well and could find anyone, was at the door.

'Ah, Nurse Vidler!'

Sister Mackintosh apologised for interrupting the conversation between Annie and the Chaplain.

'Nurse Vidler, would you be so kind as to make your way to help Nurses Mabel and Betty? We are going to be two nurses short for the night time ward rounds.'

'Yes, of course, Sister. I was just going.'

Crispen Honeybourn stood up to greet the Sister. He knew at

once that she seemed flustered, not her usual ebullient self.

'Come in, Sister. How can I help?'

'Crispen, we have a very serious problem. I don't know who I should report it to, but it must be with the utmost secrecy and discretion.'

'What is it, Sister? You look very worried and this is not like you at all. It must be something bad.'

'I'm afraid that one of the nurses has been badly assaulted. The other nurses are bound to find out and gossip will abound as well as fear.'

'Where is the nurse now?' he asked.

'She is in my room. Nurse Mabel and Nurse Betty Bell are with her. I have forced them to secrecy. That is why I was also keen to send Nurse Vidler along to help. She is a bit more worldly-wise than the others. I can rely on her.'

'Where is the man responsible?'

'That's the problem. We can't find him. He's hiding somewhere on the ship. No doubt about it. He is a very slippery character.'

'Who was it? A soldier? A sailor?'

'No, it wasn't either. It was that Maltese tenor who sang for us at the tea party. Who would have thought it?'

'Well, I am so sorry to hear about this, Sister. I did have a few reservations about the man, but I certainly didn't expect this.'

'What did you make of him, Crispen?'

He paused for a few moments to consider whether he would be speaking out of turn. He didn't know the character any better than the nurses did.

'I hope I am not speaking out of turn, Sister. I was rather puzzled. As a singer, he had excellent diction. Faultless, in fact. I do know that singers can learn this, of course. Sometimes, though, if a singer is from the Mediterranean region it is often possible to detect a lengthening of their sung vowels.'

Sister Mackintosh was flabbergasted. Was there no end to Crispen's knowledge, let alone his great sense of intuition?

'I don't think he is Maltese at all, and he isn't a soldier.'

'He must be reported to the C.O. at once. He must be found before he hurts anyone else.'

Crispen Honeybourn assumed his Chaplain's role immediately. He excused himself and replaced his official cap so as to be dressed appropriately for his role.

Sister Mackintosh hurried back to her room and the injured nurse.

Nurse Betty Bell had volunteered to remain with Nurse Wilson.

'I've had plenty of experience of patching people up, Sister. I've cleaned the wound, but I'm not sure whether it needs a plaster. She's going to have a huge bruise over the right eye.'

Sister Mackintosh examined the nurse's wound.

'You are quite right, Nurse. It is swelling. I think we will just put a loose compress on it for now. We'll keep her here for tonight. I will re-assess it in the morning. I think we should give her something to help her sleep.'

'Yes, Sister.'

'It is very kind of you to volunteer to stay with Nurse Wilson during the night. Can you manage in the chair? I will find you a warm blanket and another pillow.'

'Thank you, Sister. I will be fine.'

'You will be quite safe now that we have two guards on the door overnight. I will look in on you every hour or so.'

'What about your sleep, Sister?'

'That's good of you to think of it, Nurse Bell. I will be all right. I must find out what has happened to the culprit before I can go to sleep at all.'

Sister Mackintosh had arrived at the C.O.'s office quite flushed and breathless. Crispen Honeybourn had arrived before her.

'Hello, Sister. Here, have my seat. How is Nurse Wilson?'

'She is very shaken and bruised around the face, but she will recover in time, Crispen. Please don't ask me for all the awful details just now.'

Sister Mackintosh didn't need to elaborate any further. Crispen could tell from her face the likelihood of what had occurred. Sadly, he had been aware of situations such as this amongst the troops from time to time.

'Have they found the man yet, Crispen?'

'A search party is underway, Sister. They are combing the entire ship, so it will take quite a while. I understand that they have arrested one of the Chinese cooks. I don't know if that is in any way connected.'

Sister Mackintosh wanted to stay with Crispen until there was any news, but she was also concerned that she had left the care of the injured nurse with a junior nurse. She was also anxious to prevent any tittle-tattle between the other nurses.

'Why don't you return to your room, Sister. I will come and inform you when we have news. Shall I walk you back?'

'Thank you, Crispen,' she said curtly, 'I will manage. I expect you will be needed here once they catch the miscreant.'

'Yes, I expect I will. In cases like this I often have to act as ship's writer, especially if it is something which has to be confidential. It could lead to a court martial. Then the ship's writer will be there officially in court.'

Sister Mackintosh returned to her room to discover that Mary Wilson had been violently sick.

'Don't worry, Sister. I've almost finished cleaning it up.'

'Thank you, Nurse Bell. You have been a great help. Why don't you go and freshen yourself up? Are you quite sure you can cope with sleeping here in the chair?'

'Yes, of course, Sister. But what about the night rounds?'

'After all the work you have done today, Nurse Bell, you deserve a much more peaceful night. You are excused the wards for tonight.'

So, Nurse Betty Bell, young and innocent about many things, was certainly having her eyes opened to the adult world. When she had first volunteered, she had no real idea of how her life would be or how much it would change. Like many other volunteer nurses, all they could envisage at first was that they would be soothing the brows of fevered soldiers and hoped to make them well again. In their dreams, many of the young nurses fantasised about meeting a handsome young officer who might resemble Douglas Fairbanks, ready to carry them off on a white horse somewhere exotic. He would have lovely smooth hands and manicured nails. That would prove that he wasn't a farmworker or a man used to getting his hands dirty. Betty Bell dreamed of a young officer who would dance with her or take her for afternoon rides in a carriage on Hampstead Heath and read poetry for her.

Betty Bell made herself comfortable in Sister's chair and watched Mary Wilson until she was sure that Mary had drifted off to sleep. In the morning, she would help Mary to wash and dress in the clean uniform which had been found for her.

Thank goodness we're nearly home, Betty thought. She was anxious to know what would happen to Mary after they arrived in Southampton.

Two more days and they would be docking. There was still the worry and possibility that enemy mines, which had already claimed returning ships, might still be under the waves, waiting for them.

Mary Wilson had very few words for anyone the morning after she had been attacked. She was overwhelmed with feelings of shame, and in her heart, she knew that she would be accused of leading her attacker on.

'They'll say it was my own fault,' she told Betty, tearfully.

Betty didn't know how to reply, so she just gave Mary a hug.

Sister Mackintosh had warned the nurses not to go gossiping about Mary's misfortune, but Annie Vidler had let slip that she had seen Mary and the Maltese nurse with Bruno Fontana. Mary had seemed to be flirting, Annie had revealed. Betty Bell kept her silence even though she was bursting to ask how far the man had gone during the attack.

'Come on, Mary,' Betty encouraged her.

'Let me help you bathe and dress. I've found a fresh, clean uniform for you.'

'Thanks, Betty, but I'll manage the washing myself, ta! I'll be glad of the clean uniform though. I'm afraid I seem to have lost my shoes.'

'Never mind. I'll go and look for them, and if they're lost we'll find another pair for you.'

'It was good of Sister to let you have the privacy of her quarters, wasn't it?' Mary nodded.

Mary found it difficult to speak, as much of her face and mouth were swollen and sore. She caught sight of herself in Sister's mirror. Then the tears flowed uncontrollably.

'How can I possibly show my face to anyone, Betty?'

'You could always say that you fell downstairs.'

'Well, I did actually, except that I was pushed.'

As Betty helped Mary Wilson to dress, she caught sight of the bruising, but she said nothing.

'There, shall I leave you to do your own hair. You can use my hairbrush if you like.'

'Thank you, Betty.'

Just then Chaplain Honeybourn knocked at the door, closely followed by Sister Mackintosh.

'May I come in, ladies? I have brought you a breakfast tray. I'm afraid there wasn't a great deal of choice this morning.'

'Thank you, Chaplain. You are very kind. This will be perfectly fine,' Betty said. She had heard her Aunt Ellice use the phrase 'perfectly fine' and she remembered it.

Betty picked up Mary's soiled clothes and made room for the breakfast tray. She rolled up the dress carefully, and just then her eyes met those of Sister Mackintosh. There was a sharp intake of breath as they both looked at the dress and realised that there was indeed more to learn. Sister Mackintosh quietly took the dress from Betty.

'You have your breakfast now, Nurse Bell, and I will deal with this.'

Betty joined the Chaplain and Mary Wilson and they ate breakfast together, though Mary had little appetite. She managed to have some porridge and a mug of warm milk.

When they had finished breakfast, Chaplain Honeybourn turned to Mary and offered her the loan of his colourful walking stick.

'It might help you today and tomorrow to move around more easily, to prevent you having any more falls.'

'Won't you need it, Chaplain?'

'Oh, I am doing well now,' he said.

'What about your patient, Chaplain, the man who painted these beautiful pictures on the stick? Won't he want it?'

'We'll return it to him tomorrow night. He will manage until then. He can't move very far at all just yet.'

The nurses examined the stick more closely. Crispen hadn't had time to admire it.

'It's very pretty. Look, everyone. How delicate.'

Mary took the stick and ran her fingers along the length of it, marvelling at the colours of the flowers and the birds.

'How could the man do all this if he can't remember anything else?' she asked.

'It's obviously an innate talent which he has been able to do quite naturally. I think in his deepest sub-conscious mind he remembers many things. It may take some time before everything comes back to him. He needs a lot of patient care and somewhere where he feels safe and can relax. The brain is a wonderful part of our anatomy. I think it has ways of shutting down to re-charge, if you like.'

The group of nurses who had now gathered in Sister's room awaiting their daily instructions suddenly became silent and very thoughtful.

'Goodness, Chaplain,' said Nurse Mabel Flowers, 'you really would have made an excellent doctor.'

Nurse Mabel Flowers held back until the younger nurses had been directed to their tasks for the day. She hadn't managed to speak with Crispen Honeybourn for days, it seemed.

'Will the Royal Navy be able to tell you who the man is, Crispen? Where can you go to find out such details?'

'It will be a lot of guess work in the first instance, Mabel. If he was on *HMS Goliath* we know that he may have enlisted at Devonport, but his ship may have sailed from Chatham. I will try to visit both establishments eventually. I feel quite optimistic that I can find his identity, in due course. It may take some time. You see, Mabel, there were about seven hundred men on *Goliath*, but only about one hundred have survived. The survivors are scattered over many different hospitals around the country. They will have been transported on different ships and with a range of very different injuries.'

'How will they be able to identify him if he can't identify himself?' Mabel asked.

'I hope the navy records will contain photographs, Mabel. It could be a long, painstaking search.'

Mabel reminded the Chaplain that Patient 355 had been very badly hurt and he was still heavily bandaged.

'His face might not be recognisable when we remove all the bandages.'

'Yes, of course, Mabel. I hadn't considered that possibility. I do remember the ship's surgeon being reluctant to remove all the dressings. He just removed sufficient for the poor man to be able to see and speak. The bandages are holding his face together. I dread to think of what might be revealed when the bandages are completely removed.'

They both shivered as they contemplated the patient's possible outcome in the hands of over-worked or unsympathetic surgeons.

'Let's try and be optimistic, Mabel. They can do amazing things. This terrible war has at the very least inspired some of the greatest surgeons to be very inventive and resourceful.'

Sister Mackintosh re-joined them and overheard their conversation.

'Won't he be sent to one of the mental hospitals, Chaplain?'

The Chaplain pursed his lips for fear of what he was actually tempted to say. He took Sister Mackintosh to one side and quietly whispered his innermost thoughts to her.'

'Not if I can help it, Sister.'

'But how can you decide what's to become of him?'

'Clearly, I cannot make any kind of clinical decision. I intend to badger the medics. In fact, I am on my way now. I can't leave it until we drop anchor.'

With that admission to Sister Mackintosh, Crispen Honeybourn thought he should extricate himself from chattering with the nurses. He needed to revert to his Chaplain's role. He decided that he must try to exert as much influence as his role would allow, to secure Patient 355's safety and forward treatment. In short he wished to become, temporarily at least, the patient's sole carer. He would take total responsibility for him, if he was allowed to do so.

The last day at sea dawned. It was a grey, misty, watery dawn as the hospital ship dropped anchor. It was so early, in fact, that it was surprising to find so many of the ship's passengers wide awake.

Chaplain Honeybourn sensed the anticipation and growing sense of excitement throughout the entire ship. Those who were mobile enough were beginning to pack their meagre possessions together, even though they might still have a lengthy wait. Some of the men would be despatched to waiting trains which would take them to Waterloo Station. Waiting for them there in London would be a fleet of ambulances, known as the 'ambulance column'. They would then be taken to hospitals in London or beyond.

The paperwork for each patient caused far more headaches for the nurses than they could have imagined. Nurse Mabel Flowers was feeling near to breaking point.

'It has all been left until too late,' she explained to the Chaplain.

'Well, I expect the final medical reports could only be made at the end of the journey. The ambulances will not know where to take them without the reports.'

'So many different regiments, ranks, and kinds of injuries. I don't know how the hospitals will manage, do you, Crispen?'

'Don't worry. It will be managed, somehow. I have been told that the London hospitals will have to take twice as many patients as they have beds for.'

'Will they have to sleep on the floor?'

'I imagine the first thing will be to sort those men who are able to walk and those who will need to be stretchered.'

The Chaplain excused himself, remembering that he had a most urgent mission regarding Patient 355.

'There is something I need to do immediately. I will be back as soon as I possibly can when we can explain to the patient exactly what will happen to him when we disembark.'

Sister Mackintosh breathed a sigh of relief.

'That will be a good idea, Chaplain. To be honest with you the patient is no real trouble to us, but he is sometimes difficult to deal with. He covers his whole body and face with the blanket when anyone approaches him. He doesn't talk, except for the odd "please" and "thank you". We know he suffers nightmares.'

'I completely understand,' the Chaplain said, 'but try to bear up and just think that before very long all our patients will be safe in hospital. Perhaps some of their families might be there as we disembark.'

'They won't be allowed on the hospital trains, will they, Chaplain?'

'That is correct. If relatives appear at Southampton Dock they will be held back. I think they will be given the patient's destinations if at all possible. I think we shall encounter most relatives at Waterloo Station. I imagine we will receive a very tumultuous reception.'

Crispen Honeybourn located the Senior Medical Officer. The officer was even more confused than the nurses. He couldn't even remember who Patient 355 was and he impatiently brushed Crispen aside.

'I'm sorry, you will have to catch up with my Deputy. I have sent him to the wards with the lists. Those men who cannot carry their own papers will have the orderlies pin them to their jackets. They will be checked as they leave the ship and again in Southampton before they are put aboard the trains.'

'So my amnesiac patient is to be sent to London then, sir?'

'If that is what the list indicates.'

The officer was irritated that Crispen Honeybourn had interrupted other procedures, but then recalled that he needed the Chaplain's help.

'Come to my office, please, Chaplain. There is another very pressing matter which you will undoubtedly be able to handle with great skill and discretion.'

Seated in the officer's private room it was clear that the officer was feeling very uncomfortable as he searched for the right words to describe their predicament.

'Look here,' he stammered, 'we— we have managed to find the attacker of Nurse Wilson. He was hiding in a galley cupboard. One of the Chinese cooks is under arrest for hiding him there. They are both chained up, but since we are virtually home we cannot deal with the legal proceedings.'

'What will happen to them, sir?'

'They are both under military arrest and will be escorted off the ship by the military police. After that they cease to be our responsibility. Of course, Chaplain, you may be called at a later date. There will be a court martial, of course.'

'What about Nurse Wilson, sir?'

'Well, I hope that is where you come in, Chaplain.'

Chaplain Honeybourn looked perplexed. What was he to do now regarding Patient 355? He had no choice but to listen to the officer.

'Nurse Wilson must be escorted to her home, if she has one, or if not to the nurses' hostel, possibly at Bart's.'

'I'll see what I can do, sir.'

'Thank you, Chaplain. Now I really must go; so much paperwork to complete.'

Crispen Honeybourn was not going to allow the officer to get away so swiftly.

'Sir, before you go—'

'What is it now, Chaplain?'

'Sir, may I request permission to take Patient 355 off the ship myself. I'd like to take sole care of him, at least until he is in a suitable hospital.'

The Medical Officer became impatient, red-faced and not a little angry with the Chaplain.

'Whatever for, man? Haven't you got enough to do? The man has lost his marbles. He needs to be in a mental hospital.'

Crispen Honeybourn was shocked beyond belief at the officer's callousness. At the same time, he understood how much pressure the officer was under.

'Sir, the patient has not lost his sanity. He is suffering deep shock and depression and a loss of memory since his head injuries.'

'What makes you think the man can ever regain his mind, Chaplain Honeybourn?'

'As I said previously, sir, the patient is aware of what is happening around him. He has spoken a few words. He thanks nurses.

He recognised the acacia bush which I fell into in Malta. The most amazing thing was that he recognised the song which the tenor sang at the tea party. He hummed along a few bars of the music and then asked if it was Charlie singing. Clearly it had jogged something from the past. Since that episode the man has remained very subdued.'

Crispen Honeybourn had taken the improvised walking stick from Nurse Wilson.

'Please examine this, sir. I gave him the stick and this is what he has done with it.'

The officer took the stick and examined the beautiful decoration.

'Good gracious! How on earth did he do this amazing work?'

Crispen, knowing full well that the officer had a great interest in art, felt he was on safer ground discussing how he had encouraged the traumatised patient to draw with pastels.

'He clearly has some kind of artistic gift, sir.'

'What was the man's regiment, Chaplain?'

'He was from the Royal Navy, sir. One of the few men who actually survived the sinking of *HMS Goliath*. We have no papers or uniform with which to identify him.'

'That is what I would like to make my first priority when we go ashore.'

'That is very noble of you, Chaplain. If I give my permission for you to be his carer, for now, where do you propose to take him?'

'Well, sir, he obviously has to be properly assessed in hospital and may need some facial surgery. After that I feel he needs to be in a specialist psychiatric unit for an assessment of his mental condition. He doesn't need locking up, sir. He is not insane.'

'Very well. I will entrust him to your care. Perhaps you could take Nurse Wilson and a second nurse with you?'

'May I ask Nurse Mabel Flowers, sir?'

'I leave that entirely up to you, Chaplain. I'm not quite sure how much use Nurse Wilson will be to you and Nurse Flowers. If she believes she is assisting you and Nurse Flowers, it might be a diversion away from her own misfortune. Please keep me informed about the patient's progress, if you can.'

'Thank you very much, sir. I will go and sort out the paperwork and speak with Nurse Flowers and Nurse Wilson.'

By the time Crispen Honeybourn had secured the paperwork and discussed the proposed arrangements with everyone concerned, Sister Mackintosh had gleaned the information for herself.

The Chief Medical Officer sat down at his desk and scribbled a hurried note for Chaplain Honeybourn.

'Take this to whichever hospital your patient is assigned, Chaplain. I can assure you that the London hospitals will be in chaos. You may have to wait some time before you are seen. I have recommended that you are seen at St. Bart's, but it will very much depend on whether they can see your patient there. As it is we have dropped anchor early in the day, but we cannot let anyone disembark until we have clearance orders.'

With that warning the Chief Medical Officer showed Chaplain Honeybourn to the door.

'If you will excuse me now, Chaplain, I have much to complete.'

'Thank you, Sir,' the Chaplain said.

Chaplain Honeybourn didn't want to push the officer any further on the question of Patient 355. He had managed to obtain the all-important piece of paper. The patient would have his instructions pinned to his jacket, as did the other stretcher cases. He was still being described as Patient 355 –rescued from *HMS Goliath*, May 14th 1915.

As the morning wore on, everyone on the ship seemed to be more impatient and anxious. Groups of friends were frantically searching for each other in case they were unable to stay together. Scraps of paper were hastily swapped with addresses they hoped were still there, and tentative arrangements were shouted across the busy decks.

'Let's meet in Trafalgar Square. Christmas Eve!'

'That's not so far off now, girls!'

From time to time there were great bursts of shouting and near hysterical singing of the latest music-hall songs. It was a temporary jollity, for they were reminded that London was now under rules of semi-darkness everywhere, curfews in some rather dubious city areas, and the uncertainty that the ambulances which were expected to meet the trains might not be sufficient.

Sister Mackintosh, efficient to the last moment, was preparing patient lists with Nurse Flowers' help.

'I have no idea what will meet us when we arrive at the trains. This might be a good working plan until we see what the facilities will be.'

'Yes, Sister, I agree,' Nurse Flowers replied confidently.

Sister Mackintosh gave one of her rare smiles of approval as she considered her young nurse. Mabel Flowers had begun her life on the hospital ship as a relatively inexperienced, shy young nurse. She had little idea of the horrors she would encounter, or the great pressures and responsibilities which would be placed upon her and her other nurse companions.

'You have been an excellent nurse, Mabel. I don't give praise very often, as you will be aware. I think you will go far. I just wanted to thank you before we disembark, and also to wish you well. We will all be going our separate ways. I may have little time to speak privately with you again.'

Mabel Flowers was astonished by Sister Mackintosh's openness and her praise. She thought very quickly how she should respond.

'Thank you, Sister. Thank you very much. I have appreciated your encouragement and I hope I have learned from your experience and helpful suggestions.'

Sister Mackintosh was more than a little flushed, but soon reverted to her customary manner.

'Well, Nurse, we must get on now. We must distribute these lists to the other nurses. If we place two nurses with each dozen patients we should be able to form an orderly queue on the railway platform. We don't want any pushing or shoving, or silliness from any of the nurses.'

Nurse Mabel agreed.

'Are we taking the stretcher cases off first, Sister?'

'Yes. At least that's our idea. Of course, I can't have eyes in the back of my head. The train orderlies may have ideas of their own. I do need to ask Chaplain Honeybourn about Patient 355 and about Mary Wilson.'

Sister Mackintosh had her serious face on.

'I am assuming that you are aware of the culprit being caught?'

'Yes, Sister. What a dreadful shock,' is all that Nurse Mabel wished to contribute to that conversation. She thought it best to keep her thoughts to herself.

'Is that all, Sister?' she asked.

'Yes, thank you, Nurse Flowers. If you could just take these lists and distribute them to the appropriate nurses I would be most grateful.'

Mary Wilson was still recovering from her ordeal. She remained in Sister Mackintosh's room, away from patients and nurses. She had to remain there until it was time to leave the ship. Arrangements had been made for her to be accompanied all the way to London to the nurses' home, at St. Bart's Hospital.

'What will happen to me, Sister?' Mary Wilson asked.

'You will remain at the nurses' home until the man who attacked you is safely under police guard. There will be a trial eventually and it is possible that you may be called to give evidence.'

'What! In person? Will I have to stand up in court?' Mary looked terrified.

'I can't do it, I can't do it,' she cried.

'Do you have parents, Nurse Wilson?' Sister asked.

'I don't know where they are,' she lied.

'Anyway, Sister, I can't let them know about this. I am too ashamed.'

Sister Mackintosh gave Mary Wilson a handkerchief.

'Here, dry your eyes. No use crying about it now. You just have to learn from the unfortunate experience and make sure it never happens again. When you are feeling better you will most certainly find nursing work. All the hospitals will be desperate for qualified nurses as well as volunteers.'

Mary Wilson was ridden with anxiety and was twisting the handkerchief into knots. Sister Mackintosh took the soggy handkerchief from her.

'Look at me, Mary Wilson. I am really sorry to have to ask you this, but I must know the truth. It will go no further, I can assure you.'

Mary knew what Sister Mackintosh was going to ask her.

'Are you still — intactus?'

Mary had never heard the word before, but she knew full well what it meant. She burst into tears.

'Will they ask me that in court, Sister?'

'I don't know, Mary. I hope not. Is there anyone who could accompany you, should the need arise?'

'I don't know,' she sobbed.

'Never mind that now. You stay here and rest. I will come for you when it is time to move. I will be back very shortly. Lock the door behind me. I will knock three times when I return.'

'Thank you, Sister. I am sorry to be another worry for you.'

Sister Mackintosh went in search of Chaplain Honeybourn.

She wanted to speak with him before they disembarked. Once they were on the ambulance train there would be little privacy or opportunity.

She found the Chaplain in the ship's tiny makeshift chapel. He was with a group of soldiers, praying over their comrade who had died during the night. Sister Mackintosh sat quietly at the back of the chapel until the Chaplain delivered his final blessing. The sad group of men thanked their Chaplain and moved off quietly.

'A pity he couldn't have quite made it home, Chaplain,' said one of the soldiers, shaking the Chaplain's hand.

'Be assured he will have a special place in a military cemetery. You will be able to visit him.'

Sister Mackintosh greeted the weary Chaplain.

'You are still ministering to them, Chaplain, even now. You must be exhausted if you have sat with the man all through the night.'

'Yes, Sister, I'm afraid I did.'

'I am sorry to bother you just now, Chaplain. I needed to ask about your visit to the Senior Medical Officer this morning.'

'Well, it began rather badly. He accused me of being completely unrealistic – mad, in fact – for wanting to look after Patient 355. However, I persuaded him to give me a letter of authority. Then he asked if I would kindly accompany Nurse Wilson to the nurses' home near to St. Bart's Hospital. I am to ask Nurse Flowers if she will also accompany her. The Senior Officer has arranged places for them there and also as nurses at St. Bart's Hospital. It is fortunate in a way because Patient 355 has been referred there for preliminary medical examination. If deemed appropriate after his wounds have been dealt with, a place will be found at a psychiatric unit, possibly at Netley.'

'Won't that mean another long train journey for him?' Sister Mackintosh asked.

'How do you feel about that, Chaplain?'

'Clearly I am pleased that they will deal with his head wounds first, and then his legs. I fear he will always need the stick, or even crutches. I am filled with apprehension about the psychological issue.'

'What is it that bothers you most?'

'The initial attitude of the officer was appalling and quite unforgiveable. Other doctors may feel the same.'

Chaplain Honeybourn explained all he had observed about Patient 355 and how he was convinced that the man was really not insane at all, just without his memory. He had shown quite a few small, but revealing aspects of his personality. He was most certainly artistic. That much was revealed in his careful and most colourful decoration of the walking stick. He knew the name of the acacia bush, which Crispen had fallen into. Then there was the amazing recognition of the Handel song which he had heard during the Malta tea party entertainment.

Sister Mackintosh listened intently and agreed that the Chaplain had arrived at the correct conclusion.

'Well, Chaplain, I suggest you let the medics see to him first and then re-assess the possibilities afterwards. I can see that you are a very determined man. You will fight his corner, won't you?'

'Of course, Sister. You are as sensible and practical as ever. It is true that I do tend to over-think things. It would be easier if we knew the patient's background.'

'You will discover it, I am sure of that. One thing at a time.'

'Yes, you are quite right, Sister.'

'Well, Chaplain, I must leave you now, but here are some tablets for your patient. Give him one in about half an hour when they begin to move the stretcher cases.'

'Thank you, Sister. I will gladly attend to that. Hopefully the poor man will drift off to sleep and wake up safely on the train, perhaps even as we arrive at Waterloo.'

Chaplain Honeybourn returned to his patient to discover that the nurses had already bathed him and put him in clean pyjamas and a thick wool jumper, to protect him from the brisk sea breeze. He explained the procedure to his patient and hoped he had not started to panic.

'I will be with you all the way to the London hospital. Do you understand?' The patient nodded.

'Would you like to take the stick? You will be walking very soon, I'm sure. Then you will be glad of it.'

The patient took tight hold of the stick and half-smiled.

'Thank you, Chaplain.'

His speech faltered as he tried to say 'Chaplain', but it was quite audible. He swallowed the pill.

'Good man.' Crispen Honeybourn breathed a sigh of relief.

'This will help you to relax while you are being taken off the ship. You might even manage a snooze. That would be good.'

The time had arrived to make their way to the exit area. Crispen Honeybourn took Patient 355 in his wheelchair very slowly and chatted to him all the time, to keep him relaxed.

He chattered about the breezy weather and how excited the other passengers were becoming. Then he spotted the coaling ships coming alongside the coal ports.

'You're probably a bit too drowsy to see just now,' he said to Patient 355, 'but I can see the coaling ships coming to re-fuel the boat with coal, ready for its return journey.'

'Coal! Coal!' The patient roused and was a little agitated.

'Coa-al!' He repeated the word but it became indistinct. Sister Mackintosh was right. The tablet would make him drowsy and incoherent. He tried to lift his finger in the direction of the coaling boats, but then lapsed into sleep. It was a mystery to the Chaplain, but obviously meant something to the patient.

Nurse Mabel Flowers followed the Chaplain and his sleeping patient. She walked steadily and linked arms with Mary Wilson, who was feeling more than a little nervous.

'Everyone is looking at me,' she said, pulling her blue wool shawl close to her face. She didn't dare to look up and was glad to have Mabel's arm to lean on.

'Don't be so silly, Mary. Everyone is so excited about being home. We'll be on the train very shortly.'

Having Mabel to guide her through the busy throng meant

that Mary Wilson didn't have to look into people's faces, and she avoided seeing the military police as they escorted a group of prisoners off the ship.

Part Four

The military police marched their prisoners off in double-quick time. Amongst the disparate group were thieves, drunkards, some violent, angry men, together with soldiers who were accused of desertion in the field. They were almost certain to be tried and shot. Lurking in the deserter's group was Bruno Fontana, the singer who had assaulted Mary Wilson. *He wasn't looking so cocky and flamboyant now,* thought Mabel.

She pulled Mary in the opposite direction. They looked out over the ship's side. There was a lot of activity around the ship – the tugboats, the coaling ships, supplies being loaded. There was a lot to learn. Mary Wilson had no idea that the ship was fuelled by coal, or that coaling ships actually followed ships to warzones so they could re-fuel when needed.

After the military police had removed the prisoners from the ship and were well out of view, the mood lightened. The stretcher cases were carefully and ceremoniously wheeled, or carried on to the waiting ambulance trains. It was quite a sight as fellow soldiers, sailors and nurses cheered them as they left the ship. They were on terra firma, they were home.

Each railway carriage was made to look like a hospital ward with beds fitted end to end, or some had an upper deck of hammocks, for those patients able enough to climb into them. The most seriously injured patients were placed nearest to the train doors so they could be swiftly manoeuvred off the train at the other end of their journey.

The nurses who had been working closely together on the hospital ship found themselves dispersed among the train carriages and with new orderlies and train supervisors.

'Sister Mackintosh seems to have disappeared,' said Nurse Mabel Flowers, much to the alarm of her particular group of nurses. They relied on her so much.

Both Nurse Mabel and Mary Wilson were relieved to have been placed with the Chaplain and his special patient.

'It's very cramped though, isn't it?' Mary complained.

Nurse Betty Bell had arrived. She was full of excitement to be returning home, at last.

'Sister's coming. She's not really disappeared. It is tricky for her to keep an eye on all of us.'

'Yes!' Chaplain Honeybourn exclaimed.

'It is tricky once the train is moving,' he continued. 'The beds have been placed end to end and right up to the connecting doors, so when the train is moving there is no way through to the next carriage. Sister Mackintosh can only reach the other carriages if we stop at a station. Then she must hop off as quickly as she can, and the same if she has to do the reverse.'

Nurse Annie Vidler burst into hysterical laughter at the thoughts of Sister Mackintosh hopping on and off the train.

Chaplain Honeybourn calmed the hilarity.

'We haven't so far to go now,' he assured them, 'but it depends on whether we have to slow down for any emergencies.'

'I don't wish to sound unnecessarily alarmist, dear nurses. We all want to get to London as quickly as we can. Just try to be patient. The trains are operating to their fullest capacity. There are bound to be breakdowns of one kind or another.'

'It's getting very dark, Chaplain,' said Annie Vidler.

'Yes, it is. The guards have been instructed to dim the lights, even dim some of them altogether. It is so that the enemy cannot trace transport movements easily.'

In spite of the semi-darkness the nurses still had to care for their patients. Oozing wounds still had to be cleansed and re-dressed. Soiled laundry had to be collected and stored. The nurses became used to the putrid smells of gangrenous flesh, together with strong antiseptic solution. Some patients died on the train, and close proximity with them was distressing both for the nurses and fellow patients.

'This is a hellhole,' screamed a soldier whose wounds had turned septic. The man began to be delirious and thrashed about violently in his bunk.

Chaplain Honeybourn felt quite useless. He had only the basic first aid knowledge, but his instinct told him he had to do something.

'Sister, shall I see if there is any more iced water left in the barrel? I could at least bathe his face and neck.'

'Thank you, Chaplain. That would be very helpful. It will take a couple of orderlies to hold him down. We'll increase his morphine but it will help to cool him down first.'

The Chaplain found the ice barrel, though now much depleted. Water had been desperately needed to cleanse wounds and for drinks to swallow tablets. He managed to soak a towel through and hurried back to the delirious patient.

'Here we are, Nurse Bell. Will this do?'

'Thank you, Chaplain. He is a bit quieter and the cool towel should help.'

Mary Wilson was relieved that the carriage was dimly lit. She had managed to find a secluded corner by the medicine chest. She had been given the job of rolling clean bandages ready for use.

The train kept moving, though never at a consistent speed. Frequent short stops meant that train passengers and nurses alike felt they would never reach Waterloo station.

'We'll get there when we get there,' joked one of the soldiers. He hummed the tune of 'A Long Way to Tipperary' until someone told him to shut up.

Crispen tried to lighten the mood.

'It's good to have a sense of humour at times like this. Just think of your arrival, when it comes. You'll have a proper meal for the first time in days, and probably a nice, warm bath.'

Nurse Mabel Flowers kept her eyes on Sister Mackintosh, hoping to anticipate her next job of work. She could feel Sister Mackintosh moving into her official, business-like mode now.

'Right, Nurse Flowers. What is the situation now, in terms of mobility? Who can and who cannot walk?'

'Well, Sister, the delirious man has sadly died. Patient 355 can only manage a couple of short steps. He will certainly need the wheelchair. I think his eyesight is likely to be limited, so he is a little shaky.'

'Very well. We will have him nearest the door and he will be alighting first, probably with an orderly.'

'Yes, Sister. How will I help? I was told not to let Nurse Wilson out of my sight.'

'Don't fuss yourself,' Sister Mackintosh said with her broad Glasgow accent. 'Chaplain Honeybourn is to accompany all three of you. The orderly is only there to manoeuvre the patient off the train. He will then place him in an ambulance, which should be waiting for you at Waterloo.'

'Chaplain Honeybourn will wait with you on the platform. We expect the London Ambulance Column will call your names. You will then accompany the patient to whichever hospital can accept him. We have requested St. Bart's, but things may be very chaotic when you arrive. You must listen very carefully for your names. There will be a lot of noise on the platform. You must all have your wits about you. Listen carefully.'

'Yes, Sister, of course we will.'

Their arrival and reception in London would be highly organised, mostly by the Red Cross, who worked together with the War Office and many wealthy civilian helpers. Some of these helpers had willingly given over their large London houses to be used as temporary hospitals.

Everyone was feeling anxious about their imminent arrival into Waterloo Station. The train crept along very slowly.

Nurse Annie Vidler tried to lighten everyone's mood by comparing their present situation with their first deployment on the Gallipoli hospital ship.

'We had a lot of dying men on the ship, didn't we?'

'It was the first time I'd ever had to lay a man's body out,' Betty Bell added.

'I felt very sick when I saw all those damaged limbs,' Nurse Mabel Flowers said with a shiver.

Chaplain Honeybourn joined the group of nurses. They were all now impatient for the train to finally pull to a halt.

'What will you remember most, Chaplain?'

Sister Mackintosh had joined them for what would be their final group conversations. Even Sister Mackintosh was feeling anxious, but not a little sad that they might all be scattered across London hospitals and to a new regime.

'It might surprise you ladies that I was terrified at having to sit and pray with so many dying young men. It was emotionally draining and I was continually worried that I might be sick. In time, I learned to put my own distress to one side. I realised that I was there to do my duty to those men in the best way I could. It certainly wasn't possible to do that if I became a shivering, nervous wreck.'

'You have been a great source of strength to all of us,' Sister Mackintosh said.

The small group of nurses and orderlies had gathered there together and gave a gentle round of applause for their Chaplain. He was mildly embarrassed, but grinned.

'I shall never forget all of you. I expect you will have had all the same anxieties as I had, being faced with such horrors. So, good luck to each and every one of you. I am sure we will meet each other again before this war is over.'

Minutes before the ambulance train pulled slowly into Waterloo Station, Sister Mackintosh and her nurses lined up together and, one by one, gave Crispen Honeybourn a polite kiss on his cheek. He in turn kissed each one by the hand. That was, all except for Sister Mackintosh, who shook him by the hand as vigorously as any sergeant major would have done.

'I hope to see you at St. Bart's,' she said softly.

'I hope so, Sister,' he smiled the broadest smile.

The train suddenly jolted them all out of their rather sentimental reverie.

There was a long, deafening screeching of brakes as the train ground to a halt along the platform. The nurses and patients saw and felt the great clouds of steam, and the most nauseating smell of soot mingled with the smells of still gangrenous wounds and dried blood everywhere.

Sister Mackintosh warned the nurses that theirs wasn't the only train to arrive that night.

'They always arrive at night to avoid the daytime commuter rush, but also to avoid them seeing the terrible sights that we have had to deal with. I dare say you may still see some awful cases from the trains, but remember – *my* nurses don't faint, they don't panic and they don't have histrionics!'

The heavy train doors banged deafeningly as they were flung open, and the train orderlies leapt out on to the platform, waving their lists and shouting names. It was all matter of fact and swiftly dealt with for the most part.

'Bearers 1 to 6, this way. Follow me,' the orderly yelled.

The bearers were to carry the most injured stretcher patients. Still they had to line up in a queue to be directed to their ambulance.

'Bearers 7 to 14, you're to Kingston. Make sure your patients are securely strapped in. It's a long ride. It is also rather dimly lit along the route.'

'Bearers 15 to 20, you're with the Chaplain and one nurse. The other nurses to follow in the next ambulance. Both to St. Bart's.'

The chief bearer couldn't locate Sister Mackintosh, so he gave Chaplain Honeybourn the report on Patient 355.

'I'm sorry to say, sir, your patient has developed a very high temperature. He is a bit delirious and hasn't had enough fluids since Southampton. Good luck, Padre.'

Sister Mackintosh came running just in time before Crispen and Patient 355 would have been sent off without her.

There was a good deal of confusion placing the other nurses in the next few ambulances. Many of the patients had not had their wounds dressed for several hours and were bleeding through, in some cases. Without Sister Mackintosh to supervise they had to use their own initiative about who would travel with which patients and who would take charge. It fell to Nurse Flowers to organise the nurses. She was worried that she might lose sight of Nurse Mary Wilson now that the Chaplain had gone ahead.

Nurses Mabel Flowers and Betty Bell travelled together and Annie Vidler kept a close eye on Mary Wilson. There was an underlying feeling that, given the opportunity, Mary Wilson might very well try to abscond into the night.

As the nurses looked back towards the platform and before the ambulances were securely locked, they saw many hundreds of men pouring off the trains. By then a sizeable group of people from the general public were also arriving at the station. They were onlookers, along with hopeful family members. Perhaps they might catch a glimpse of their sons, brothers, husbands or other family members, returning safe from the war.

'Keep back, ladies and gentlemen, please,' the guards shouted.

'Let us deal with the ambulance column first.'

The public were soon herded behind barriers. They continued to shout and wave. They cheered as each patient was placed in an ambulance.

The patients who could respond, waved back to the crowds.

'Good luck, chaps,' someone shouted and the cheering continued. The crowds stayed there until all the soldiers had either been placed in ambulances or were able to walk away by themselves.

It was a miracle that any of the well soldiers or sailors were able to find any of their welcoming relatives, but many did. It was a pattern that would be repeated night after night, bringing thousands of men home.

'What will happen to men who haven't got a family waiting for them on the platform,' Betty Bell wondered, aloud.

'Some will find their way to the Forces Clubs. There are plenty of those around all the stations,' one of the orderlies explained.

The orderly's companion smirked.

'I guess there'll be plenty of ladies willing to put them up for the night?'

The orderlies chortled as they moved away to complete their

task. There would be a quick turn around for the trains once all the passengers had gone, and the trains had a huge clean up, ready to bring more men home again.

At last they were on terra firma, and Sister Mackintosh could breathe a sigh of relief. The other nurses, the patients and returning troops each had their own priorities. So did Chaplain Crispen Honeybourn. He could think of nothing else but seeing his special Patient 355 safely installed in the hospital where he would be treated without further delay.

'It shouldn't be a very long journey,' he assured them all, 'but it is very dark and we may not be able to see which way we will be going. It's my guess that we will be going over Blackfriars towards St. Bart's.'

The ambulance driver didn't speak. He was overtired and had to really concentrate on the road before him. All the city lights had been dimmed, or switched off entirely. He couldn't afford to have an accident whilst driving hospital patients. The driver would be greatly relieved when they reached their destination. It was his tenth journey of the night and he wasn't finished yet.

It had been a long, exhausting day for all the train's passengers. Returning troops, patients and nurses were willing themselves to stay awake now they had finally reached home. Outside there was little for them to see, and the motion of the ambulance and its warmer atmosphere lulled some of them into a short-lived sleep. That was, except for Mary Wilson.

'What will happen to me when we arrive?' she asked her friend, Nurse Mabel Flowers.

'Stop worrying, Mary. What I expect to happen and what will actually happen could be quite different.'

Mabel was already feeling irritated by Mary. Although she sympathised with her situation, she didn't want to be totally responsible for her. She had her own life to pick up again. That would be hard enough.

'Chaplain Honeybourn will register his patient first. Then he will accompany both of us to the nurses' home nearby. We will be able to have a rest before we report to the hospital tomorrow morning.'

'It's almost tomorrow now,' Mary yawned.

'Yes. I know it is, but we will be able to sleep for a few hours in a clean, comfortable bed. Hopefully we will be able to have the luxury of a proper bath before we have to report for duty.'

'Ah, bliss,' said Mary, 'a proper bath. I don't think I will ever feel clean again.'

In the dimness of the ambulance it was impossible to see Patient 355 properly, but Mabel felt his forehead just as they were stepping out of the ambulance.

'He's burning up. We need to move him quickly!'

Sister Mackintosh and Chaplain Honeybourn saw that the patient was safely transferred to the stretcher-bearer without delay.

The Chaplain shouted to Nurses Mabel and Mary.

'I will catch up with you as soon as I can. Perhaps you can find seats in the hospital lobby?'

He was forced to join a lengthy queue, though his patient was whisked away to an emergency ward immediately. He wasn't happy to have lost sight of him, but Crispen did realise how important the documentation was.

Sister Mackintosh realised the dilemma. She was also anxious to make sure everyone was in the right place. She paced up and down impatiently, backwards and forwards. It seemed an age before Crispen was seen. He managed eventually to deposit the required documentation with officials.

He hurried to find the emergency ward. Sister Mackintosh followed on behind, leaving the two nurses to wait in the hospital lobby.

'Here he is, Chaplain. He is surrounded by ice blocks to cool his temperature. The surgeon should be here to assess him within the hour.'

The two nurses had found a seat in the lobby and were intermittently dropping asleep. Sister Mackintosh volunteered to sit by the patient until the surgeon arrived.

'Thank you, Sister. I will see the nurses to their lodgings and I will return immediately. Then we will sort something for you. I am sure you have been awake for twenty-four hours!'

'I shall be happy for a sit-down. The ward Sister has brought me some tea. I will enjoy that. Off you go, to do your duty, yet again.'

Sister Mackintosh gave Crispen Honeybourn one of her rare smiles. It was a genuine smile of deep appreciation, coupled with relief that they had all arrived home to Britain, unscathed.

That was, except for the hapless Mary Wilson, and of course Patient 355, whose different nightmares might never disappear.

Sister Mackintosh was persuaded by the Night Sister to take turns with her sharing a mattress in the Night Sister's office. They would each do two hours on duty and two hours off through the night.

Crispen Honeybourn dutifully escorted his two nurses to the safety of the nurses' home, nearby and wearily made his way back to the hospital. Tiredness creeping over him and with his thoughts racing through a multitude of issues, he stumbled. In the darkness, he had taken a wrong turning. He had to double back to find his bearings.

'Lost your way, dearie,' he heard a voice say.

A small, wispy figure of a woman appeared from a nearby doorway. She stubbed out a cigarette on the doorpost.

'Are you looking for lodgings for the night, love?' the woman said.

Crispen was alarmed. He was being propositioned.

'No, no, thank you,' he stuttered, 'I am on my way to the hospital.'

'You sure I can't offer you a nightcap, or something else?' she drawled.

He quickened his pace. He could feel his heart thumping.

'O, God, help me,' he cried out.

He could see the hospital gates, not far in the distance.

The woman disappeared. By the time Crispen reached the

hospital, his pulse was racing and he had broken out into a nervous sweat. Safely inside the gates he paused.

'Crispen Honeybourn,' he chided himself, 'what an idiot! After everything you've been through and you couldn't deal with the situation without being upset. Fancy invoking God's help!'

He put it all down to extreme exhaustion.

By the time he reached the emergency ward, Sister Mackintosh was asleep in the Night Sister's room. Patient 355 seemed to be sleeping peacefully, probably for the first time in months.

Crispen was completely shattered. He fell asleep in the chair beside the patient's bed.

Crispen remained there in the chair for the duration of the night. He had failed to notice that his patient, who had been swiftly attended to a couple of hours before, had been sedated and re-bandaged. They would both have a peaceful and pain-free night.

The next morning, just as dawn was beginning to break, Crispen was the first to wake. He realised that he was still fully clothed in the uniform he had been wearing for the previous two days. He desperately needed a bath and a shave, though he had no idea where his razor might be.

The Night Sister showed Crispen to the doctor's private bathroom. She found him a razor and some fresh soap.

'They won't mind,' she told him.

Crispen felt so much better after his warm bath, ready to face the world again. He would have to think and plan his next movements carefully.

He was offered breakfast in the nurses' dining room. It was a simple meal of scrambled eggs, toasted muffins and a pot of tea, which he drank from a china cup. It felt wonderful and so civilised, especially after his months away. He appreciated being on land again. He hadn't realised just how unstable he had felt being on a ship for so long, and then the train journey. Crispen totally understood Sister Mackintosh's delight at being on terra firma again. It meant feeling more in control of one's own body.

Crispen Honeybourn felt as though he was a new man, newly

energised after his breakfast and luxurious bath. He would wait to speak with the surgeon and his Patient 355 before following his own plans. *How lovely it would be,* he thought, *to just have a leisurely walk through one of the London parks.* It would be a great thrill, perhaps another day. It would be an indulgence when he had so many other things to attend to.

First things first, Crispen, he reminded himself. He had to register himself at the Union Jack Club. Then he needed to report to his superiors in the army chaplaincy. He had no idea whether he would be required to travel abroad again. He wasn't even sure whether he would want to repeat his experience. He had a great deal of thinking to do. With a month's accumulated leave Crispen Honeybourn would have time to think.

He knew without a shadow of doubt that he wanted to use his leave to help the patient he had been caring for since Gallipoli. It was his only mission and he would be single-minded in order to accomplish it. He felt quite sure that if he could uncover the man's identity it would aid his recovery. Though he was not medically trained, Crispen could only search, hope and pray for the best of results.

Crispen's first job that morning would be to buy a new diary notebook. His Chaplain's official diary had become very soiled with dirt and sea spray. That was unsurprising when he considered where the diary had been.

The Chaplain's diary was a most precious and important record of his time ministering to soldiers and sailors, and to nurses and doctors, stretcher-bearers, even other chaplains. There were many sad pages where he had recorded details of many deaths and burials on land and sea. There were lists of names and home addresses of parents and families whom he felt obliged to inform of their losses. Sometimes he had managed to send messages home from dying soldiers. It was sometimes extremely distressing work, but Crispen felt honoured that he had been able to do it.

Yes, his new venture would most certainly need a new notebook. The pages of his former diary were not just full, but were coming loose. He would attempt to repair the old pages and then the diary would be placed somewhere safe. After the war, there would be many diaries written as testament to the madness of mankind.

Sister Mackintosh greeted him.

'Good morning, Crispen. You were awake very early this morning. Have you breakfasted?'

'Good morning, Sister. Thank you, I have had a very delicious breakfast and an even more wonderful relaxing bath. It would be good now if I could have some fresh, clean clothes. I hope to rectify that shortly.'

He explained that he was hoping to speak with the surgeon again before travelling to Portsmouth.

'I shall arrange for a room at the Union Jack Club. I will do that this morning as well as sorting out my travel warrants.'

'What then, Crispen?' Sister Mackintosh asked.

'I have a month's leave, Sister. I intend to visit the navy in Portsmouth. I really want to find this poor patient's identity. I am quite determined. Everything else will wait.'

'You are indeed a truly kind man, Crispen Honeybourn, giving up your leave to help a relative stranger.'

'I am convinced if we can find out who he is we may be able to locate his family. Then, who knows, he may begin to regain his memory. If he doesn't, then at least we will have tried. His family may wish to look after him.'

'What if you can't do that?'

'Everything is possible, Sister, with… ' he paused.

'With God's help, Crispen?'

'I was about to say… with patience and perseverance. It's knowing where to look first. Don't you agree?'

Sister Mackintosh nodded in agreement, though she wore a slightly puzzled look. She had never questioned Crispen's motives or his character beyond the visible role he displayed as a conscientious Chaplain. He always carried out his duties with a seeming calm confidence and dignity. She admired him for that. He never panicked or became outwardly angry.

At least that was her impression of the young Chaplain. He had the patience of a saint. He looked like a man of God to her. Of course, she had not seen the panic in Crispen's face the previous evening when he had been approached by a 'lady of the night.'

She hadn't heard him shriek, 'God help me!'

Crispen Honeybourn was most certainly an enigma. Here he was putting 'his patient' before any consideration of his own traumatic experiences in Gallipoli, in Malta and now in London. He had no relatives of his own and no place to go home to. Still, he did not seem to be downcast. He was simply driven to do his best in whatever way he could, wherever he found he could be of use.

'Come, Sister. I see the surgeon is on his way. He has quite an entourage of young doctors with him. I don't want to miss anything important.'

They both hurried to join the surgeon's group. Sister Mackintosh held the bundle of patient records and charts, not wishing to trust them to a junior nurse.

'This is Patient 355, sir. No name, as yet.'

'Thank you, Sister. I am pleased to see that his temperature has come down slightly. You will notice that I have managed to remove the mass of caked-on dried blood. In one sense, it has held his flesh together, but there has been infection and he will be terribly scarred.

'We will keep his facial wounds under close observation and cleansing daily, before we decide what more we can expect to be able to do for him in the future. Surgeons are finding their way with plastic surgery, but it is very much a case of trial and error. There just isn't one simple answer. Some of these men have very complex damage.'

'Sir, can you tell us anything about his legs?' Crispen asked.

'The legs are healing fairly well, though the left leg was not properly set in Malta, I'm afraid. He will always walk with a limp. He will need crutches. I am sorry to say there will be no more soldiering or marching, for him.'

'Sir, we believe he was a sailor, rescued when *HMS Goliath* was sunk, in May.'

'Well, in that case, the young man is fortunate to be alive at all. I know about the sinking. So many lives were lost.'

'One more thing, sir. What will happen about his mental care?'

'Chaplain. I recognise your concern. As you see we are completely overwhelmed here with surgical cases of every kind you care to consider. We just cannot deal with the mental problems as well, other than sedation. What I can do is to refer your patient elsewhere, hoping there will be a place. Possibly to Netley. I understand there are some good psychiatric doctors working in Edinburgh, but that is a very long way to go.'

Chaplain Honeybourn listened carefully.

'I am afraid there are many thousands of potential psychiatric patients. Some treatments aren't successful and the psychiatrists themselves are divided in their opinions. I suspect that treatments in this field are still very much trial and error too.'

The Chaplain thanked the surgeon for his time and his explanations.

'Come and see me again, Chaplain, when the patient has more physical strength. Then we will consider referring him elsewhere.'

Sister Mackintosh was very impressed.

'This surgeon usually works through the ward like a whirlwind, not stopping for discussions. Well done, Crispen.'

'Thank you, Sister. I've written it all down.'

Patient 355 was still not fully awake, or focussed.

Crispen Honeybourn tried to rouse him.

'Can you hear me?'

'Yes,' the man whispered.

'Listen carefully to me. Sister has all the details of the surgeon's assessment of your condition. You should feel a little more comfortable soon, now they have re-bandaged you. I must go away for a few days. I have written down everything that I am going to try and do for you. Sister will look after it for you. You can read it when you are feeling better. Do you understand?'

The patient nodded.

'Sister Mackintosh will look after you, and Nurse Mabel

Flowers will be here for you today. Do you remember Nurse Mabel?'

The patient, now wide awake, nodded again and gave Crispen a half-smile. That half-smile heartened Crispen's spirit and resolve. If the patient could give a half-smile such as that with such a badly damaged face, he would smile even wider once he recovered fully.

'He will probably need reminding about me, Sister,' Crispen edged towards the door, not wishing to make a fuss.

'I will keep my eye on him, don't fuss.'

'When are you off to Portsmouth, Crispen?'

They were out of earshot of any other staff, so Sister Mackintosh was able to use his first name, as if they were off duty.

'Right now,' he said. 'That is, when I have acquired a clean set of clothes. I have reserved a room at the Union Jack Club to use on my return.'

Without any thought to where he might stay once he arrived in Portsmouth, Crispen Honeybourn set off with high hopes and determination. It was still quite early in the morning when he boarded the train at Waterloo. He had an officer's travel warrant and was shown to a first-class compartment. He couldn't help thinking how very different this was, compared to the ambulance train. He expected the train would soon fill with passengers, both military and general public. He nodded off to sleep for a while. It was certainly more comfortable than the hospital chair had been the night before.

Crispen had slept through the clanking of the train wheels through Clapham Junction. By the time he woke up the train had stopped at Wimbledon station to pick up some businessmen travelling to work somewhere further down the line, perhaps in Weybridge or Woking. He should have brought a rail map with him. He had forgotten all the station names. No matter. He remembered the journey through parts of Surrey. Then it would be Hampshire.

Crispen loved Hampshire and the Surrey countryside, away from the towns. It was autumn now, and seeing the glorious colours of the trees and hedgerows reminded him of Keats's poem. He was trying to remember all the words, but kept mixing up one line with another. He remembered the famous line of course, *'seasons of mellow fruitfulness'*. How lovely that was.

The train stopped at Guildford where his peaceful journey was interrupted. There was quite a lengthy wait as the train filled with soldiers and sailors. They were either off on their first postings as new recruits, or they were returning troops who had been home on leave for a short time. Crispen could recognise the new recruits. They were all fresh-faced and eager, with little understanding of what they might be facing. The returning troops were quiet and rather sombre. They would have just left their wives and children behind and may already be feeling homesick. There was little in the way of eagerness in their faces, and only reluctant conversation, even in the officers' compartment.

Eventually, with the motion of the train to help him, Crispen drifted off to sleep again. He must have slept through at least two or three more station stops. When he woke, he realised that they were now in Hampshire and his compartment was full of naval officers. On the platform, he observed many more naval ratings, bound for Portsmouth and Southampton.

Far from feeling his usual optimistic and hopeful self, Crispen Honeybourn felt a great sadness that many of these young men would either be travelling back on a hospital train, or maybe not at all. It was easy to feel a sense of despair, considering his earlier experiences.

In the field of battle and often against all the odds, he had witnessed young soldiers, filled with bravado, or at least a philosophical outlook, to help them cope.

'If your name's on it, chum, that's it!'

Few of the men said they believed in God, or thought they would be guided safely through if they prayed. Crispen remembered talking with men who knew they were dying. Often, it was then they would ask for a prayer and a blessing, which he gladly gave.

It wouldn't be very long before the train would arrive in

Portsmouth. Crispen closed his eyes, not sleeping, just thinking. He knew no one in the compartment and, unusually for him, he hadn't attempted to begin a conversation with anyone.

At last the train slowed down as it approached the station. There was a great deal of movement and noise as the soldiers and sailors picked up their kitbags. As they stepped off the train they checked their uniform. Some of the young first time recruits felt uncomfortable wearing their regulation headwear, but had been made very aware of the rules about proper dress. They could be punished if they were found to be improperly attired.

Crispen held back and allowed the troops and the officers to go before him. He had arranged transport for himself. Someone, a navy driver presumably, should be waiting for him. He was rather anxious not to become embroiled in the great melee of troops. He didn't want to find himself in the wrong place, as he had done in Gallipoli.

On that occasion, he had found himself on the wrong ship and became a chaplain to sailors mostly, but also to soldiers from the trenches. Reflecting on that experience he had been grateful for the friendships he had formed with the nurses. For the first time in his life he had someone to write postcards to.

He truly hoped that he would have good news to share with Mabel Flowers and the other nurses, not forgetting Sister Mackintosh. *How different his life had become because of a quirk of fate. Or could it have been meant to happen?* he wondered.

Crispen Honeybourn stopped daydreaming and looked for his driver once the bulk of the troops had cleared the platform to board their trucks.

He spotted the driver standing by his jeep. He waved and the driver responded. Crispen felt very privileged as the driver saluted him. Crispen responded.

'Off to Devonport, sir. Is that correct?'

'Thank you, driver. I have a room booked at the Sailor's Rest. Do you know it?'

'Yes, indeed I do, sir, but wouldn't you be better staying in officer accommodation on the base?'

'Thank you, driver. I shall be fine. I will be visiting the base tomorrow. I expect I shall only be here for a couple of days. I would appreciate a lift to the base tomorrow, if possible.'

'Yes, sir. It has already been booked for you. It may be myself, or it may be a different driver. These days our set routines can change at short notice.'

'I understand that, driver.'

They arrived at the Sailor's Rest and the driver limped round to open the jeep door for Crispen.

'You're limping, driver. I hadn't noticed that before. Have you been injured?'

'Yes, sir. I was with the West Surreys. They brought me back from France with a broken leg and pneumonia. It was touch and go for a while. I was luckier than some of my friends. I'm alive!'

'So how are you still here in Portsmouth?'

'I came back on a hospital ship and was hospitalised in Portsmouth. I've nowhere else to go so I stayed once I was well enough to drive again. I'm a civilian now, honourable discharge. I'm not sure what was honourable about it though, sir.'

Crispen shook him by the hand and asked his name.

'My name's Stanley, sir. George Stanley.'

'Well, thank you, George. I hope I will see you tomorrow.'

George Stanley saluted Crispen Honeybourn again and Crispen responded.

Part Five

Crispen Honeybourn had heard about the Sailor's Rest hostel. He knew its reputation as a temperance hostel near the Devonport dockyard and its partner hostel in Portsmouth. Sailors could have a meal, a bed for the night and a bath, or short-term lodgings. It suited men who had been on leave, or returned from war and were awaiting new orders. Many did not have a home to go to. Crispen soon realised that this was a real home from home where the men didn't just lodge, but received much in the way of personal care and sometimes had their simple medical needs, such as chiropody and dental issues, dealt with. Sometimes there were sailors who just needed to talk about their experiences. Others were so upset, even traumatised, by events abroad that they just wanted to escape for a bit of peace and quiet, by themselves.

The warden welcomed Chaplain Honeybourn to the Sailor's Rest and was very proud to talk of its history and how the public now valued the work of this sanctuary.

'Even Queen Victoria was impressed, sir. She endowed a cabin and, as a result, we now receive some important funds to keep us going. Her Majesty allowed us to call it the 'Royal Sailor's Rest'.

Crispen Honeybourn was impressed.

'Follow me, sir. It's a pleasure to welcome you here. I'm afraid it is quite basic, but it is clean and you can be assured of a good supper. You can come and go as you please, but I must ask that you leave your key at the desk if you go out.'

'Supper is served between 6.00 p.m. and 10.00 p.m. If you would prefer to have something light you can choose a sandwich and soup. I can have it brought to your cabin if you prefer not to sit with the sailors.'

'I am very happy to sit with the sailors, warden. It is part of the reason why I am here.'

Crispen decided to keep the real reason for his visit to himself for the time being. The warden, being quite an astute man, suspected there would be something important on the Chaplain's agenda. It wasn't often that military chaplains or padres actually stayed at the 'The Rest', though religious services were a regular part of the routine.

'We often have visiting chaplains or padres, sir. They give talks on a variety of topics, not always religious. After the talks the men have the opportunity to sign the pledge that they would refrain from drinking alcohol.'

Crispen Honeybourn stifled a grin, as did the warden.

'I think the idea is that the many facilities offered to the sailors would help them to combat alcoholism and prevent them from causing harm or mischief on the streets around the dockyard.'

Having settled Crispen in his 'cabin', as the rooms were called, the warden offered to show him all the facilities.

'Here is the lounge, separate from the dining room,' he explained.

Crispen thought it all looked very civilised.

'We are particularly proud of our noticeboards. We try to update them daily. We explain all the facilities on offer, but it is also a way of sailors being able to communicate with other sailors. I'm afraid the 'Missing' board seems to grow daily.'

Crispen Honeybourn was very impressed with the care shown at every part of the Sailor's Rest.

'Finally, sir, I would like to show you our library area. We have a group of dedicated ladies who volunteer weekly. They bring books, newspapers and sometimes religious tracts, courtesy of the Temperance Movement. If the men don't want to read anything they can play cards or dominoes. If they want to play darts or billiards they have an area to themselves.'

The warden relaxed when he realised that Chaplain Honeybourn was not there to secretly inspect the premises or to write reports on the way it was being administrated. He seemed genuinely very interested in the sailors as individuals in need.

'What have we here, warden?'

'Ah, yes. Sorry I should have explained this corner. This is probably one of the most useful things we can offer.'

'The men can avail themselves of free writing paper and envelopes, with stamps,' he explained. 'They can write to their wives or other relatives or friends. Of course, not all of them are literate. Some of them are helped by our magnificent volunteer ladies, who write for them, if they so wish.'

'That is really wonderful. It must be very difficult for those men, especially if their families have been displaced because of the bombings.'

'Yes, indeed, sir. Many areas of London have copped it. We have many sailors who are distraught because they cannot find their families.'

'How do you begin to help?' Crispen asked.

'With a good deal of tact and sensitivity, sir. We feel ready and able to help in many ways, but we mustn't presume how they feel. They must be allowed to find their way for themselves. You will see what I mean, sir. Look here.'

Crispen was amazed to see a huge board ruled into columns and with headings. Each heading indicated the kinds of help the men could request. They were invited to tick anything they felt in need of.

'I see the most requested help is with letter and postcard writing, then finding addresses and travel details. Money issues, telephone messages and placing adverts in newspapers. The list seems endless.'

'We will have to add another board for this section, sir.'

Crispen read the many messages under 'MISSING PALS'.

'Yes, sir, the men can pick up a postcard from the desk. They write the names of anyone they wish to find. We keep their details on file for them and they hope someone will come forward with news.'

'And do people come forward?' Crispen asked.

'To be honest, sir, we usually get letters and cards from men who are lying injured in a hospital somewhere. They know that they can write here and we will do our best to let their comrades know where they are.'

'So you are an unofficial post office?'

'Yes, I guess we are, though sometimes I must say it is a bit upsetting for us to see the same man who comes time and time again for weeks on end and he has no news.'

Crispen Honeybourn was filled with admiration for all the welfare work and genuine care being given to the sailors at Devonport. He decided it was time to be open with the warden of the Royal Sailor's Rest.

'Actually, Warden, I am here on a mission myself.'

'I knew there was something, sir.'

'Let's take a comfortable seat here, Chaplain.'

They found a quiet area where they would not be disturbed.

'I am on a mission to discover a survivor's identity,' he confided.

'The man was badly injured when his ship was sunk in the Dardanelles. He has head and facial injuries as well as two broken legs. Sadly, as a result of such horrific injuries, the man is not only traumatised and fearful, but he has no memory to speak of. He wore nothing with which we could identify him and we don't really know whether he will fully recover. I sincerely hope that I can spend some time trying to locate his family.'

The warden listened intently.

'It isn't the first time I have heard this kind of story, Chaplain. What a dreadful tragedy it was. I understand that almost the entire crew were lost – hundreds, in fact.'

Crispen revealed that he had been on the hospital ship as a military chaplain, when the man in question was brought on board. Both men fell silent with their thoughts.

'I will be visiting the personnel and recruitment offices tomorrow. They should have crew lists, with photographs, which might provide some clues.

'Didn't *Goliath* sail out of Chatham, sir?'

'I'm not sure, but this was a very young man. He would have had to undergo initial training in Devonport, I think. I do hope we have the right place. It is where I was directed to look. If not there will surely be records elsewhere.'

'I wish you the best of luck, sir. You are obviously a very determined and dedicated man. Please let me know if you find his name. We can place it on our boards. That way we may come across other survivors who might have known him. So far, I have to say we have not seen anyone from *Goliath*. I fear that of the men who did survive, many will still be hospitalised all over Britain. Most were taken initially to London, we are told. Some will then have been transferred elsewhere, even sent home if they were sufficiently recovered.'

'That's if they had a home to go to.'

'Yes, of course. Thank you, warden. I think I should turn in now. I need a really good sleep.'

'Would you like a mug of cocoa? I will bring it to your cabin if you wish, sir?'

'Thank you. I would appreciate that very much. It will help me to relax.'

It was Crispen Honeybourn's first night of uninterrupted sleep in many weeks.

He was so grateful to have found the Sailor's Rest. He understood completely how the sailors who stayed here would regard it as a safe, welcoming place, a second home for many. Crispen imagined that had he the luxury of being able to stay longer he would be able to completely relax. He could benefit from the fresh sea air and long walks along the cliffs and coast. He would see the ships and they would remind him of his own difficult experiences of the past few months. He drank his cocoa and stopped daydreaming. He had an important job to do before he could even contemplate anything else. He felt lucky to have survived.

Crispen Honeybourn enjoyed his breakfast in the congenial

company of the young sailors. He would have enjoyed staying longer to talk with them. They had such stories to tell. He bade the sailors farewell, as his driver George Stanley had arrived promptly, as promised.

'Good morning, Chaplain, sir.' George Stanley saluted Crispen, as was customary, even though George was technically a civilian. He remembered his military etiquette.

'The Youth Training School, is it, sir?'

'Yes, thank you, George. That's the first stop anyway. We might have to go elsewhere after that. Will you be available?'

'I can wait for you all day, sir, if you wish.'

It was just a short drive to the Youth Training School.

Security was paramount. Crispen and his driver were stopped at the gates and were required to show their identity papers.

'What is your business here today, sir?' the guard asked.

'I have permission to consult sailors' records of service,' Crispen explained.

'Very good, sir, and is this man your official driver?'

The guard examined the driver's papers, even though he knew full well who the driver was. He saw the man every day. Nevertheless, rules of security measures were tighter than they had ever been. The guard had to observe everything down to the very last detail.

George Stanley grinned as the guard gave him a wink as he opened the gate to let them through into the base.

'They think we might be German spies, sir, looking to steal our operating codes.'

Crispen's eyes widened with disbelief.

'Really! Are you pulling my leg, George?'

'No, sir. We've had all kinds of stories about German spies infiltrating the navy bases.'

George Stanley left the Chaplain at the Records Office, where again Crispen had to produce his identity papers.

'I will come back in an hour and wait for you outside, sir. If you need any longer the desk officer will come and give me a message.'

'Thank you again, George. I am very much obliged to you.'

'Gor, blimey, fancy that!' George said to himself. 'None of the officers I have met have ever spoken to me like that.'

The way the Chaplain had spoken to him made him feel good. It made him feel useful. Driving was all he was fit for now.

'Maybe,' George thought, 'when this wretched war is over, I'll be a London cabbie. It won't matter then if I have got a gammy leg.'

Crispen Honeybourn had expected the Personnel Records Office to be a quiet place, full of ledger books and files and junior officers seated at desks, completing paperwork. He was surprised to discover it was a bustling hive of activity. Clerks were running backwards and forwards with papers of every kind. He couldn't have imagined the enormous piles of records of every kind. There was everything from birth, marriage and death records to medical reports, court martial reports, as well as timetables, sailing details and supplies of equipment and victuals.

Crispen's appearance was considered an extra irritation they would rather have done without that morning. Still, they had generously supplied him with a desk in the corner of one office and the services of a junior clerk/runner whose job it would be to fetch and carry any files which might be useful to Crispen's research.

The reception area was rather crowded and fraught.

Crispen Honeybourn had no idea that boys as young as fourteen were still being trained and therefore would be correctly processed through the navy records offices. A distraught mother was arguing with the desk clerk.

'You've already sent one of my boys to his death. I don't want you to have this one too,' she pleaded.

The boy desperately wanted to enlist and he argued very tearfully with his mother.

'The training takes at least twelve weeks, Ma. The war might be over by then. I could be home by Christmas.'

'I don't want you coming home in a box,' she screamed.

The clerk was becoming exasperated. Crispen Honeybourn, the onlooker, understood both sides of the dilemma.

The clerk ushered Crispen away from the arguing mother and son.

'I'm sorry, sir, for that awkward moment. Please come with me. I will see to the lady and her boy shortly.' The debacle had left Crispen waiting for almost half an hour, and he was aware that his driver was still waiting outside. He scribbled a short note for George Stanley, asking him to return at lunchtime.

'Please would you be so kind as to pass this to my driver? There is no way I can complete my task quickly.'

'Yes, sir. I certainly will. Here we are, sir. We have put you in this corner, and here is your clerk/runner for the day or as long as you should require him.'

The clerk introduced a very pale-faced, nervous-looking young man. He looked no more than a schoolboy. He had bright red hair and a mass of freckles. He was unsure whether he should salute a Chaplain. Crispen took the initiative and shook the boy by the hand.

'How do you do? It's very kind of you to come and help. What should I call you?'

'My name is Harry Abbott, sir. I am going to be trained as a navy writer.'

'How old are you, Harry Abbott?'

'I'm seventeen, sir, almost eighteen.'

Crispen smiled.

'With a name like that perhaps you come from a long line of priests?'

'I don't rightly know, sir. I doubt it!'

'A navy writer. Well, that will be a fine career for you.'

'Thank you, sir,' the boy relaxed.

Crispen Honeybourn was good at helping people to relax. He had broken the ice with his clerk/runner. He settled himself at the corner desk. It was with some sense of optimism he laid out his special notebook diary and spare sheets of paper and pens.

He was going to get along very well with Harry Abbott. The young man had stopped fidgeting and shaking with nerves. He had been prepared with the details of Chaplain Honeybourn's mission to find the identity of the amnesiac Patient 355, who was still lying in a London hospital bed, with no idea of who he was.

Harry Abbott was an intelligent and quick-thinking young man. Crispen had been told that Harry had memorised practically all the locations of thousands of records held in the establishments offices. Crispen Honeybourn was very grateful for the help of Harry Abbott, who might very well have to trudge through several corridors and climb many stepladders in search of crucial bits of information.

Crispen had developed a slight cough and he felt a distinct chill coming on. He should have brought a thicker jumper to Devonport. He hadn't accounted for the fact that he would feel much colder nearer the coast.

Harry Abbott brought a small mug of tea for the Chaplain.

'You'd better drink it quickly, sir. We aren't supposed to have drinks in here.'

Crispen grinned as he sipped the tea.

'Are you a rule-breaker, Harry?'

'Not usually, sir, but I could see you were shivering. It's not too warm in here, is it?'

'That's very thoughtful of you, Harry.'

'Well, I'm new here so I can say I didn't know the rules. Anyway, everyone is very busy. No one will bother us. Don't worry, Chaplain. I won't tell any fibs.'

Crispen finished the tea and Harry swiftly returned the mug to the canteen. He was eager to get started.

'Here I am now, sir. What can I do to help?'

'Do you know, Harry, I don't really know where to begin. It's like looking for a needle in a haystack.'

'Well, if I may, sir, I suggest you write down everything you do know first. Then the ideas will come. How would it be if I made the first list, while you concentrate on remembering any of the details, even small ones? It is difficult sometimes to write and think at the same time, isn't it?'

'You are quite correct, Harry. That is how we will start.'

'Beg pardon, sir. Would it be good to look at the official crew photograph of *HMS Goliath*, taken just before she sailed?'

Harry had found a copy of the official photograph. It was impressive to see the entire crew in their full uniforms and white caps. The problem was that the crew of seven hundred or more men were so small on the photograph it was almost impossible to see their close features. Many of them looked alike.

'I'll see if I can get it enlarged, bit by bit,' said Harry. 'It might be well worth a shot.'

'There is no hurry. We need to do as you suggest and write down the things we do know for sure.'

'O.K.,' said Harry, pencil poised. 'Tell me what the man looks like as far as you can.'

'Well, I estimate he is about 5' 3" tall and very slim. He has black hair, straight, black hair and a very pale complexion. It is difficult because much of his face and head is still swathed in bandages.'

'What about his body? Has he any birthmarks or tattoos?'

'Not that I was aware of.'

'You said that his legs were broken?'

'That is true, but of course that wouldn't be on any of the photographs we have here.'

'No, but his medical records will be forwarded and they will all be added to his file eventually.'

'What about his arms and hands? Are they muscular? Does he look as though he might have been a keen sportsman?'

Suddenly Crispen Honeybourn had a positive flash of clear recognition.

'His hands! His hands, of course!'

'What about the hands, sir?'

Crispen related the story of the makeshift walking stick.

'The man borrowed my pastels when I was away somewhere. I returned to find that he had decorated the stick in the most

135

beautiful coloured birds and flowers. Somehow, from the depths of this very traumatised young man, he instinctively remembered how to draw.'

'Very probably the most important thing I can remember about the episode is that after we washed to pastel dust from his hands I saw that all his fingertips were permanently stained, dark brown in colour. The ends of his fingers were rather rough, especially on the right hand.'

Harry Abbott sat back in his chair and beamed with joy.

'What is it, Harry?'

'Sir, Chaplain Honeybourn, without knowing it you may very well be on the trail. I am guessing, sir, but this is a man who works with his hands, a skilled man. He wasn't an engineer, or a sailor as such. I would like to suggest that he will have been one of the artisan group of workers.'

Both of them remained silent for a few moments. There were deep intakes of breath before either of them spoke.

'How can we find who were the artisan group of workers?'

'That's easy, sir.'

'So we scour the crew lists?'

'Well, it might be simpler and quicker to find the artisan lists and then consult the huge crew list.'

Crispen was completely out of his depth with naval knowledge, but he was learning fast.

Harry Abbott left Crispen Honeybourn alone with his thoughts for a few minutes. He went in search of crew lists and lists of the artisan workers who had sailed with *HMS Goliath*.

Harry Abbott had already worked out in his mind which section of workers they were looking for, but he wondered if it would be a good thing for the Chaplain to realise for himself. He returned with all the lists they would need.

'Here you are, Chaplain, sir. See what you can find here. The different trades are listed first, like an index. It details which page you will need for each trade. It is sometimes difficult for us landlubbers to realise how big these ships are and how many workers they need to keep everything in the best condition.'

'Yes, I see each trade has its own "crew". I had no idea how many plumbers or coopers they would have needed. Then there were blacksmiths, shipwrights, painters and... and... ' Crispen was lost for words.

'... and carpenters!' Harry finished the sentence for him.

'Harry. Have we found him? Is this it?'

'It is very likely that we have, sir. But we still have a list of names to play with and let's be reasonable. We are working on a great deal of guess work here.'

'Yes, Harry. I do realise that. We still have much to do. How are we doing for time?'

'Don't worry about the time, sir. The day shift people will disappear, but you will notice newer clerks about the place until quite late. Can I ask one more question, sir. What age do you think your man is?'

'Well, that is another difficult question. He looks quite young, though I would guess he is a few years older than yourself, perhaps twenty or so.'

Harry perused the photograph once more.

'We could eliminate all the older-looking men. That might narrow it down a bit, but it is still like looking for a needle in a haystack. I do have another idea, sir. Did you hear the man speak at all?'

'Very few words, so far, but he was beginning to make an effort. He stuttered quite a bit and managed to thank the nurses sometimes.'

Crispen remembered that awful morning when the nurses had tried to use the bath-trolley by his bedside.

'He was terrified when he saw his reflection in the water. He screamed out loud "Charlie". It was obviously a flashback to the sinking of the ship.'

'Is there anything else, sir, anything which might help us to identify a regional accent at all?'

Crispen thought long and hard.

'There was that time when we were in Malta. I had an awkward accident when I fell into a prickly bush, taking some of the flowers with me. It was really strange how the man recognised the flowers. "A-a-ca-cia," he said and then crumbled the flowers in his hand. That was all he would say.'

'What about the accent?'

'I'm not totally sure, but I would certainly say he was from somewhere in London, not a cockney accent though. I would hazard a guess that his family might be fairly upper working class, perhaps white-collar, if you know what I mean?'

Harry was beginning to form a picture of the patient.

'Did he show an interest in anything else around him?'

Crispen recalled the tea party given by the soldiers at the Malta hospital.

'It was a rather strange experience. It was very moving and rather surreal.'

Harry was listening intently and writing everything down.

'Between all the music-hall songs and banter we then had a quieter rendition from a singer, a tenor who sang Handel's 'Silent Worship'. For several bars of the music our patient was quietly trying to hum along with it. He only managed a couple of the words and he stopped when he realised that we were listening to him.'

'We have quite several pieces of the jigsaw now, Chaplain. Let's stop and try to put the facts in some kind of order.'

'Yes, Harry. We have a lot of the pieces, though they don't connect just yet. This is how our man is living day to day. He seems to have flashes of light or a feeling, an instinct, but nothing tangible so far.'

Harry Abbott consulted his watch.

'Chaplain, sir, may I suggest before we continue that you meet up with your driver. He will be waiting outside as it is just about lunchtime, as you arranged.'

'Yes, of course. Thank you, Harry. I can't believe how the morning has passed so quickly.'

'We can resume after a break, if you wish, sir. I could continue the search for you. I am sure you are ready for a rest?'

Crispen had developed a painful crick in his back and stood up very slowly.

'I guess it was due to my sleeping in a strange bed last night,' he said, forcing a smile.

He asked Harry if there was anywhere close by where they could eat.

'Yes, sir, of course. Would you like the officer's mess?'

'Where do you have your meals, Harry?'

'I mostly use the sailor's tavern, sir, but that might be a bit rough for you.'

After a few moments of jollity and mild embarrassment it was amicably decided that Crispen Honeybourn would take both Harry Abbott and George Stanley, his driver, to the sailor's tavern where he would treat them both to a meal.

'You both deserve it,' he said. 'I am very grateful to you for your time and willingness to help. I have a strong feeling that we may be able to solve the riddle of my amnesiac patient.'

The sailor's tavern was rather dark inside, it was smoke-filled as this wasn't a temperance hotel, and it was rather noisy as sailors were joking and laughing as they related their tales to each other. It was all good-natured, especially as some sailors were a touch inebriated. It wasn't the sort of place that Crispen would normally frequent, but he was happy to observe the scene.

Both Harry and George were well aware that they were on official duty time. They were not inclined to order anything stronger than a pot of tea.

George would usually eat bread, cheese and pickle at lunchtime. It was a quick meal and he was never quite sure when he would be required to drive, or even wait somewhere for hours. He was quite used to cooking for himself in the evenings.

He often made a pan of stew which would last him for a few meals. It wasn't always easy to find meat in the shops so when he did manage to buy a bit of beef, or a rabbit, he regarded that as a special treat.

Harry Abbott lived at the Youth Training Establishment for now, so he was at the mercy of the navy cooks there, unless he could afford to eat at the sailor's tavern.

Crispen Honeybourn perused the slate menu at the bar. The landlord was not used to seeing military men of the cloth in his bar. He hovered in attendance and gave the bar counter an extra special clean.

'Good afternoon, Padre, is it?'

'Well, it's Chaplain Honeybourn if we want to be precise, landlord.' He gave the landlord one of his infectious grins.

'I beg your pardon, Chaplain. We don't usually have the pleasure of your colleagues in here. They mostly eat with the navy officers in their mess.'

Crispen decided not to engage in a lengthy conversation about his other colleagues over the bar.

Harry, George and Crispen each decided that a fish meal would be much appreciated, so that is what they ordered.

'I will bring it over to you as soon as it is ready, Chaplain, sir. You'll find the window seats most comfortable.'

'Thank you, landlord. I am much obliged.'

The landlord made haste to the kitchen with the order, *'much obliged'* he repeated to himself with a smile and a little skip. It wasn't often that he heard people speaking so politely.

Crispen surveyed the sailors around him. It was becoming noisier as more arrived. He was developing a headache, along with feeling shivery. He guessed that he would rally after he had eaten something. He was surrounded by some raucousness and colourful language, but he didn't mind when they burst into singing sailor shanty songs. It was quite a treat, really, though Harry and George both wondered what the Chaplain would make of it all.

Crispen's mind was elsewhere, thinking of his patient still lying in hospital at St. Bart's. He wondered if the nurses had kept reminding him of Crispen's mission, on his behalf. He hoped that the man wouldn't be moved elsewhere before he returned to London. Although Crispen would only have been away for three days, perhaps four, it might seem longer to the patient who had begun to respond to Crispen's gentle approach and presence. All Crispen wanted then was to get back to the office and put the pieces of the jigsaw together. He was relieved when their meal arrived.

'Here we are, Chaplain, sir, young gentlemen. Enjoy your meal.'

'Thank you, landlord,' Crispen said.

'It smells delicious,' said Harry.

'I will enjoy this, thanks, landlord,' said George.

Conversation between the three men was polite, though rather limited. Harry, aware that he mustn't speak with his mouth full of food, and George, always aware of knowing his place. Harry Abbott was sure to be an excellent officer one day. He seemed to Crispen to be a model military man. He was intelligent, quick-thinking and very conscious that he should not discuss anything of a military nature except with his immediate superior's permission. Chaplain Honeybourn was a unique case. Harry only felt comfortable speaking with the Chaplain in the privacy of their temporary office.

Crispen Honeybourn was oblivious, for once, as he could only focus his thoughts on the possibility of success in his mission.

Harry imagined that there would be many more men who had suffered what was being described as shell-shock and would maybe lose their memory. One thing he was sure of was that there would not be too many men like Chaplain Honeybourn to look after them.

George Stanley was more familiar with army officers and soldiers. He knew very little about the workings of the navy secretariat, but he was learning day by day how things were done. He wasn't particularly curious to know exactly what Harry and the Chaplain were investigating. He was just glad to be alive, even with a bad leg.

George was happy that he could still drive for a living. If necessary, he would be able to turn his hand to repairing cars or trucks. There wasn't anything that George didn't know about engines. If he didn't instantly know how to solve a mechanical problem, he would soon find out.

Even as a young boy George would take things apart to see how they worked. Then he would put them back together again. Maybe after the war he would be able to save some money for a vehicle of his own. He was quite certain that to be his own man, with his own vehicle, meant freedom. He would be able to go anywhere he liked. He didn't want to be tied down with a wife and family like some of his army chums. He had no family to go home to now, so he had become quite used to fending for himself. He liked it that way.

The tavern was emptying as the sailors who had to return to work made their way back to their offices or ships. There were a few small groups of men huddling in corners, talking quietly about their experiences. Some were awaiting new orders, but Crispen sensed that many of them felt aimless, in some sort of limbo. Others were on leave but had nowhere to go. The landlord was keeping a close eye on them. It wasn't good for his trade if they were to become troublesome.

Crispen was anxious to return to his continuing quest.

'O.K., gentlemen, are we all ready to move?'

Harry Abbott and George Stanley thanked Crispen for their lunch and they were more than ready to return to the important work in hand. George agreed to return at 6.00 p.m. to drive Crispen back to the Sailor's Rest. He would spend one more night in his cabin there before making the train journey back to London.

Between them, Crispen Honeybourn and Harry Abbott compiled list after list, sometimes becoming sidetracked. They listed the names of all the painters, carpenters and shipwrights from *HMS Goliath*, as they felt sure that was where they would find their man.

Then they made a list of all the sailors who were named Charles, or Charlie. Charlie was the name Patient 355 had screamed that day when the nurses had brought the bath-trolley next to his bed.

Crispen had guessed that because the patient had used the name 'Charlie' and not Charles then he would have been more familiar with the man. It was reasonable to suppose that they were friends and certainly closely working together. Crispen related the moment when the patient had heard the singer at the Malta tea party.

'He asked if it was Charlie singing.'

'Of course, sir, it may well be that Charlie was not a tradesman at all.'

'Yes, I had considered that, Harry. All the men named Charles amongst the artisan lists are much older. We are only assuming that they were of a similar age.'

'We will have to think of another way. What if we look at the original crew list?'

'Sir, there will be hundreds of names to go through.'

'Well, let's make a start. All you need is a ruler and a steady hand. Keep it steady down the page and stop each time you find the name Charles. We'll do half each.'

Crispen hoped it wouldn't be another wild goose chase.

Whilst Crispen was very determined, he realised that they had very little real evidence to go on. They pressed on. With Crispen's intuition and Harry Abbott's clear thinking they would be sure to unravel something.

They worked steadily down the columns looking for anyone named Charles, or Charlie.

'I am surprised, Harry. We've looked through about half the ship's crew and only found a few named Charles. Most of those are officers and not tradesmen or craftsmen.'

'There are plenty of Arthurs, Alfreds and Edwards.'

'Yes,' grinned Crispen, 'I guess many of those would be named after Queen Victoria's children.'

Convinced that they were on the right track, they worked steadily on until they reached surnames beginning with the letter 'R'.

'Sir, look here, what about these two?'

Harry could hardly contain his sense of excitement.

He read slowly.

'Charles Henry Ramsay, leading signalman, date of birth

January 4th 1883, Honiton, Devon. Next of kin… mother. There is an address, sir.'

'What about the other man, Harry?'

'This one has two addresses, Sir.' He read, 'Charles Richards, Third Writer, date of birth: May 13th 1894. Next of kin Alfred Richards, father, Kensington and Alice Coombe, aunt, living at Old Vicarage, Highgate.'

Crispen Honeybourn couldn't believe his ears. He sat bolt upright in his chair.

'Read the last one again, Harry, please.'

Harry read more slowly and clearly. Crispen's hands couldn't stop shaking as he took the paper from Harry, to read it again for himself. He looked in disbelief.

'Harry. This has to be divine providence.'

'Sir,' Harry wasn't quite sure what Crispen meant. 'Do you wish me to carry on down to 'Z', sir?'

Crispen Honeybourn could neither speak nor move. He felt frozen to his seat.

'Are you ill, sir?'

'No, Harry. I am in shock. I will explain to you later. Yes, I think we should carry on, just in case we miss anything.'

There were only a few more men named Charles. Most were older men, but Crispen didn't want to accidentally discount any one. It might be an assumption too far.

They checked the missing, presumed drowned list and there was Charles Richards' name. Crispen didn't know whether to feel elated because of their find, or disappointed that they had spent such a long time looking for Patient 355's details, without success. He felt immensely sad for the Richards family, but didn't want to embarrass Harry with his own involvement in this family.

'I once knew the Coombe family,' he confided to Harry.

He would say no more, for fear of becoming overwrought himself. *Chaplains were meant to keep a cool head and think of others,* he told himself.

'Perhaps the family will be able to enlighten you, sir?'

'I will most certainly pay them a visit after this, Harry.'

Crispen wrote all the details he would need in his very special notebook diary. He thanked Harry profusely for his time and all the concentrated work he had helped him with.

'I do hope you will find the patient's name, eventually, sir. Will you let me know when you do?'

'I most certainly will, Harry.'

As Crispen Honeybourn bade farewell to Harry Abbott, memories of his early life came flooding back, but not in any particular order.

This, of course, would be exactly how Patient 355 was seeing things in his mind's eye – disjointed. The patient's flashbacks were minute and fleeting. Crispen would be able to piece more of his life together. One forgotten memory would re-surface and that memory would lead to another. His own jigsaw puzzle would be easier to complete.

Crispen spent a mostly sleepless night, tossing and turning in his cabin at the Sailor's Rest. He couldn't help the thoughts churning over and over in his head. Much of his early life was rather hazy, but now he was having to remember. He had to continue the search. This time it wasn't just for Patient 355. It was also for himself. Eventually, he slept.

Crispen Honeybourn was relieved to be aboard a very early train to London. He remembered very clearly the ambulance train he had travelled on before. He managed to have a quiet seat in a first-class compartment. He closed his eyes, pretending to sleep at first, then he did fall asleep properly. He was exhausted after the continuous tossing and turning, trying to sleep the night before.

He woke up when the train lurched to a stop at Guildford. There weren't so many soldiers travelling in the direction of London. The soldiers on the train looked as though they might be on leave. He needed to pull himself together now. He had almost forgotten that he had a room reserved at the Union Jack Club. It would be very nice to have a bath, a good sleep and some new clothes to wear. He would have to think really carefully about how he would contact the Richards family.

Crispen Honeybourn felt as though he had been away from London for much longer than three days, so much had happened. He would be relieved and glad to get back to St. Bart's to see how Patient 355 was progressing. He thought of the hospital nurses who were having to adjust to life in a 'proper' hospital again, on terra firma. He hoped Mary Wilson had recovered from her ordeal. Sister Mackintosh would be much happier and in her element in St. Bart's, even though all of the nurses would be working night and day till they were exhausted. Most of all he had missed the gentle Nurse Mabel Flowers. Just then he felt a little embarrassed that he still had the remainder of his month's accrued leave. He was free to do as he pleased. His mind wandered through several frivolous possibilities, but in truth there was only one thing that he had a burning desire to do. He wanted to begin his mission immediately.

Crispen had deliberated whether he should continue his pastoral work in the hospital and forgo his leave, but he reasoned that if he were to use the time helping Patient 355 recover his identity, nothing would give him greater satisfaction. Of course, Crispen couldn't possibly know, or even guess, whether recovering his identity would also help him recover the rest of his memory.

This was certainly uncharted territory for Crispen. He had read many works, as much as he could find written by experts in the field of psychiatric medicine. Unfortunately, it had only served to confuse him as he had read many conflicting ideas. The treatments offered to depressed patients seemed very haphazard. Soldiers suffering from nervous illnesses, sometimes called 'shell-shock' or even neurasthenia, appeared to be receiving widely different treatment, or none at all. In some cases, Crispen thought the treatments were quite brutal.

He could only reason that the doctors were overwhelmed with such cases. Most of them seemed to be doing the best they knew how. They were overstretched in terms of hospital beds and were often short of nurses who found themselves going from ward to ward and constantly tired. The war had presented them with unprecedented numbers of patients to care for. It was no wonder that even the specialist hospital at Netley, near Southampton, struggled to cope with diverse mental issues. Crispen had heard of some excellent work being carried out at Craiglockhart Hospital, in Edinburgh. But that would be a very long way to send his patient, even if he did fulfil the criteria for admittance.

Crispen thought about his own training as a theology student. He had also studied psychology. He felt that he probably knew as much about the human psyche as many of the young doctors. He had certainly spent more time talking with soldiers and sailors. He felt momentarily slightly ashamed of himself for feeling rather smug. He hadn't meant to feel smug. It was just that he had always been fascinated in what motivated people to behave in the ways they did.

Mental dysfunction was an altogether different area of expertise. He wanted to learn all about it. He wondered whether he might be able to take a sabbatical year, in order to study psychotherapy properly. He would give that idea some very careful thought. He really needed some time to assess his own motivation for remaining within the chaplaincy.

The train pulled into Waterloo station and his mind had to focus on the present and the practical things he had to do.

He was glad to leave the train. The walk up to 91 Waterloo Road – to the Union Jack Club – was just what he needed, but the walk took longer than he remembered it. The air was cool, even in London. Winter was not very far away. It reminded him that he must buy a proper coat, for the winter months. His summer uniform was adequate for the Mediterranean, but not for London. Should he buy an army coat, or a black wool coat, more fitting to the clergy?

'Do you have luggage, sir?'

The concierge at the Union Jack Club was surprised that Crispen had so few belongings with him. He explained that he had previously booked his accommodation and he had deposited his travel case in the club's safe room.

'I'll just get that for you then, sir. Will you be needing a reservation for dinner this evening?'

Crispen hesitated for a few moments.

'Not for this evening, thank you. I must get back to St. Bart's Hospital. I'm not sure when I will be returning. I will get something to eat at the hospital.

'Very well, sir. Here are your keys. Would you like me to take your luggage up for you?'

'No, thank you. I will manage myself.'

Crispen found the lift, though if his room had been situated on the lower floors he would have taken the stairs. He didn't care for being in lifts or rooms on upper floors. London was still a target for zeppelins. He was as nervous as everyone else, since the zeppelins didn't seem to give much warning. He expected to hear about the Germans bombing London when he arrived at the hospital. He reminded himself that he needed to be acquainted with fire drills, just in case.

He unpacked the clothes which had been squashed into his travel case amongst his books and papers. The case hadn't been unpacked since leaving the hospital ship, so the clothes were crumpled. Only his khaki jacket which had been folded neatly on the top of everything else was anywhere decent to wear. He gave the jacket a good shake and placed it on a hanger in the bathroom. He hoped that by having a hot bath himself the jacket might look refreshed after hanging in the steam for a while.

The hot bath did wonders for Crispen's aching limbs. It helped him relax enough to feel ready for his next visit to St. Bart's Hospital. His jacket miraculously also shed most of its creases. He gave it a further vigorous shake and hung it near to an open window. The jacket wasn't too damp. It would do.

Usually, Crispen was quite frugal, but on this occasion, since he was extremely tired, he thought it expedient for once to take a cab to the hospital. First, though, he would try to buy a camera in one of the shops on the Strand. He might have to go as far as Fleet Street.

Having satisfied himself that he was as clean and smart as he could be, Crispen Honeybourn checked, as usual, that he was carrying his official documents, his identity card, hospital pass and cash in his wallet. He set off to find a camera.

It would be very nice, he thought, to have photographs of the nurses he had worked with on the hospital ship and in Malta. It had been a truly frightening and harrowing time for all of them. He didn't want to forget anyone, but his other motive was to have pictures ready, if and when Patient 355 did manage to recover his identity.

Spurred on by the hopes of that happening Crispen wanted to have photographs of the patient he was trying to help. He hoped, too, that should he find the man's family he would be able to show the pictures to them also. He would have to be very sensitive about the photographs. He would talk with Nurse Mabel Flowers and Sister Mackintosh. They were both very sensible about things. Mabel would help him.

Walking through London streets towards the Strand was a revelation to Crispen. The happy, cheerful and unhurried London that he remembered from pre-war days had disappeared. People were rushing everywhere. Groups of shouting anti-war protesters and women suffragettes, who were shouting even louder were being told to move along. Policemen were exasperated as the groups just started shouting and waving their banners somewhere else. Crispen couldn't hear everything but he did hear something about anti-conscription meetings. It seemed that forced conscription was not far away.

Crispen felt pained by seeing so many sad and angry faces. There were soldiers too, some hobbling along on crutches, stopping occasionally if they could find a free corner to beg for money or cigarettes.

Once more Crispen was overcome with feelings of personal inadequacy.

He managed to find a cheap box-type camera and some film in one of the tobacconist's shops. He was sure that he had been over-charged, but he didn't make a fuss. He was glad to have the camera.

He searched for a cab, but there were none to be found. He risked getting on a bus and hoped it would be going in the direction of West Smithfield. He noticed the sky darkening quite quickly. Soon it would be much darker, especially with the lack of street lighting. He would have to plan his return journey to the Union Jack Club. It wasn't an easy walk. Maybe the streets would have cleared a bit by then and perhaps he would find a cab more easily.

The patients and doctors were having their supper when he arrived at St. Bart's. Sister Mackintosh had, apparently, taken her break with the doctors. Nurse Mabel Flowers was in charge.

Mabel's face lit up when she saw Crispen.

'Chaplain, welcome back. We have missed you.'

'No need to call me Chaplain, Mabel. At least not when we are alone.'

He closed the door so that they were alone. Then, like an excited schoolboy, he clasped her hands in his.

'Mabel, I have so much to tell you. I hardly know where to begin. Let us sit down, but first you must tell me about Patient 355. How is he?'

'He has missed you, Crispen. He kept looking around for you. We, that is, Nurse Vidler, Nurse Bell and myself, have attempted to encourage him to talk a little.'

Crispen nodded and smiled.

'Good, very good, Mabel.'

'We asked him if he was looking for the Chaplain.'

'Did he reply?'

'He repeated, "Chaplain, Chaplain." We tried it again the next day and he said it again. Just the one word, Chaplain.'

'Has he said anything else, since then?'

'No, but he has done something quite extraordinary. You'll never be able to guess.'

Crispen shook his head.

'He has drawn a sketch of you. A good likeness. He won't part with it. He keeps it folded in his pyjama pocket. We have spotted him looking at the picture and putting it away again, for safety. I think it is the most incredible step forward for him Crispen. What do you think?'

'My guess is that he is using the picture to reinforce his memory of me. He knows that he has a problem.'

Crispen asked if the doctors had made any decisions about his future treatments.

Mabel pursed her lips. She had learned to do as Sister Mackintosh did when she wanted to show her disapproval, but without speaking.

'I heard one doctor talking about hydrotherapy at another hospital, but there was some disagreement.'

'They mustn't do that to him, Mabel. What can we do?'

'I agree, Crispen. It sounds like shock treatment to me. I am convinced he can be helped in a more humane, gentle way.'

'How much time have you got just now, Mabel?'

'Not long. A few minutes. Then Sister Mackintosh will be back.'

'Will you take me to the patient?'

'Of course I will, Crispen. Are you going to the ward in your uniform?'

'Yes, is that all right? No time to fuss with white coats. Of course, this is my khaki jacket. I am officially an army chaplain. I just found myself on the wrong ship, so I ended up serving sailors as well as land troops.'

Chaplain Honeybourn sat quietly beside his patient. He watched him sleeping after his supper. Nurse Mabel explained that the head bandages were being changed daily. As the flesh wounds were healing over they could now see a little more of his facial features.

'He is going to have some awful scars, Chaplain.'

'Maybe he will, Nurse Mabel. Still, you know there are some amazing surgeons who are having some success with skin grafts.

The mental scars may prove to be more problematical, I fear.'

The patient roused from his sleep, even though the Chaplain and Nurse Mabel were whispering quietly together.

Nurse Mabel plumped up his pillows and raised him up.

'There you are, that's better isn't it? Look who is here to see you?'

'Hello, old chap. How are you today?' the Chaplain greeted him.

The patient smiled. It was the first time they had seen him smile like that. He struggled to speak. After a couple of stammers, he managed to say, 'Chap-chap-lain.'

His hand went to his pyjama pocket and he took out the folded paper. He handed it to the Chaplain.

'Goodness me. I can't believe you have made a picture of me. How on earth did you manage it?'

'Re-re-mem-ber you.'

'I am very touched that you chose me as your subject. It is a good likeness. I am even more pleased that little by little you seem to be recovering.'

Nurse Mabel struggled to contain her tears.

'Shall I go and leave you with him, Chaplain?'

'No, not at all. In fact, I have an idea. I wonder if you would like to help. I have bought a small camera. I would like to take a photograph of our patient with each of us. He will be able to look at the photograph and remember both of us when we are not here.'

'I'd be glad to help, but you will have to show me what to do, Chaplain. I have never used a camera before.'

'It's easy. Look, you hold it like this. You look at the subject here. You must keep the subject in the centre and keep the camera very still. When you are happy with the picture you press here. You must keep the camera very still until after the shutter has stopped. Let's do a practice one first.'

'You take the patient by himself and I will guide you.'

Nurse Mabel's hands were shaking.

'Never mind, you will be calmer on the second try.'

Chaplain Honeybourn encouraged her, and the second attempt was indeed more successful. She even managed a third time.

'Well done, Mabel. Sorry, Nurse Mabel.'

'Perhaps you should save that remark until you see if the pictures are all right,' she joked.

'Now Nurse Mabel. I will take a picture of you with the patient and then we will let you have another go with my face in the picture.'

The patient grinned. He pointed to his face.

'Not good face.'

'That doesn't matter just now,' the Chaplain told him.

'I would like to use the pictures to see if I can help you to find your family. Would you like me to do that?'

They had no idea of how the patient would respond, but it was necessary to ask him that question.

The patient looked hesitant and worried but couldn't find words to express his feelings. At least, not yet.

'Never mind just now. We'll talk about that later?'

The patient nodded. Nurse Mabel urged the Chaplain to let him rest now.

'He is still very confused and frightened, Chaplain, but I know he is improving. He was so pleased to see you. The drawing he produced was like a miracle. His potential to remember is not totally lost.'

'I feel the same as you, Nurse. Unfortunately, neither of us are experts. But the question remains whether the experts can do any better?'

Nurse Mabel Flowers shuddered as she remembered a conversation she had overheard between two psychiatric doctors.

'They were advocating freezing cold baths for him.'

'Did they say when?'

'No, Chaplain.'

Some of the junior nurses had returned to the ward for their night shift. They were gossiping about the Chaplain and Nurse Flowers spending so much time together. Nurse Annie Vidler tried to stop the chatter.

'Don't be so silly, you lot. The Chaplain and Mabel have known each other for a very long time. Their interest is in helping Patient 355 recover his memory.'

'He is still in deep shock after Gallipoli,' Annie said. 'Anything that reminds him of the explosions that terrible night in May when most of the ship's crew were drowned or blown apart puts him in a deep panic and confusion.'

'How can the Chaplain help his memory, Nurse Vidler?' asked one of the young nurses.

'I don't honestly know how he can help, Nurse. I do know that the Chaplain is working jolly hard, in his own time, to try to find the man's family.'

'I think the Chaplain is a wonderful man,' the nurse said.

'So do we all,' chorused the other nurses.

'What's all the chatter here,' boomed Sister Mackintosh's voice. Sister didn't wait for a reply. 'Have you all had your supper yet?'

'No, Sister,' was the unanimous reply.

'Well, off you go, and quietly, please. I shall expect you all back here in half an hour.'

'Yes, Sister,' they mumbled.

Finale

Crispen Honeybourn felt optimistic that they had achieved quite a breakthrough with the patient that day. He was now aware that he needed to make his way back to the Union Jack Club before the street became too dark for safety. He certainly didn't wish to repeat the experience he'd had when he took a wrong turning that dark night when he had encountered a lady of the night.

'I will say goodnight to you nurses. I will try to get a cab before the streets are too dark.'

By the time he had reached a major road, the skies had become quite dark. He hailed the first cab he saw, without hesitation. It seemed a frivolous expense on that occasion, but he deemed it to be a wise choice. He would be back in the Union Jack Club in plenty of time to sort out his itinerary for the next day. He had a niggling feeling of guilt that he hadn't managed to visit the church nearest to the hospital. St. Bartholomew the Great had narrowly escaped being obliterated by three zeppelin attacks which had occurred nearby. He would visit another day.

The first task for the next day was to have the photographs developed. Then to work on an itinerary which would give him a valid excuse to be in the Highgate area. He wasn't sure about the wisdom of it. He would sleep on it and make a decision in the morning.

Crispen Honeybourn was still thinking about his mission the next morning. He must have been subconsciously trying to unravel things all night long because he woke with a pounding headache.

It was only to be expected, Crispen thought. He too was experiencing flashbacks, shadows of his early life. He was remembering fragments of his early childhood, though nothing in great detail. Some things were clearer than others. He tried to remember the earliest time when he was given a temporary home at Highgate Vicarage. He was only five years old then, and very likely he was remembering things which other people had told him. It was sad that he couldn't remember his parents who had died in a deadly influenza epidemic. Reverend Coombe had lost his wife in the same scourge. Crispen was given a home with Reverend Coombe and his two young daughters, Frances and Alice, who were a little older than he. They were mostly looked after by the housekeeper and a maidservant.

Crispen remembered Reverend Coombe as a quiet, kindly man who had a long white beard. He thought he had come to live with Father Christmas. Crispen smiled at the thought. He vaguely had a memory of Frances, the eldest girl, who could be very bossy one day and friendly the next. He was rather wary of her. Alice, on the other hand, who was nearer his own age was a much gentler playmate who included him in whatever game they happened to be playing. It was Alice who first helped him to read. The world opened up for Crispen after that. He loved books and there were plenty of those at the vicarage. Reverend Coombe was happy for him to read any of the books on the shelves. He loved books about history and geography. He imagined how it might be to live in Africa, or other lands where there were exotic animals.

By the time he was ten, Crispen was sent away to school, according to his father's wishes. It was a school for sons of the clergy.

Crispen's memories were clearer of that period of his life. He had liked learning, but it wasn't such a happy time with some of the other boys. After living with girls it came as somewhat of a shock to discover just how boisterous and cruel some boys could be.

Crispen had never really played any kind of sport, other than garden tennis with the girls. That was quite fun. They had no proper rules, only the ones they made for themselves. Crispen, being rather short-sighted, had just entered into the spirit of the game and lobbed the ball back and forth, just hoping it had gone over the net. The girls took it all in good spirits. The boys at school did not.

He stopped daydreaming and got on with the business of the day. Crispen found a specialist shop near to Fleet Street.

'I can have them done for you tomorrow afternoon, sir, say about 4.00 p.m.,' the assistant said.

'Very well, thank you. I will be here.'

Crispen was disappointed not to have the photographs the same day, but he would just have to be patient, and wait.

At least the wait would allow him to think more clearly about how he was going to approach Highgate Vicarage. He found a small café on Fleet Street and a secluded corner by himself. He had time to think. There were so many questions to deal with.

Should he telephone the vicarage first? Would it be more correct to send a note, or a telegram? Which day of the week would be best? Would they even remember him? It was a very long time ago. It would be presumptuous to expect them to remember.

Thoughts whirled round and round his head. First he had a plan. Then he didn't. He tried again and couldn't seem to find the appropriate words.

The morning soon passed and the café became noisier. It was obviously a lunchtime meeting place for young reporters. Their voices became louder and louder as they shared their stories with each other. Crispen was fascinated and could cheerfully have stayed to listen to them. It had reminded him of his student days when groups of students would argue together. It was all very good-natured. No one lost any friends over their conflicting opinions. It was a happy time. He wondered how many of his fellow students would have parishes of their own. How many had become military padres or chaplains? How many had wives and families?

There were times when Crispen would have appreciated the comradeship of other clergy. He had felt a bit of a loner, even on the hospital ships. He had enjoyed the company of the nurses, of course, but it was not quite the same thing as being able to discuss things as one chaplain to another.

He did recall Mabel Flowers once asking him a very direct question, which took him aback.

'Do you speak with God?' she had asked.

'I mean, apart from saying your prayers?'

He had found that question impossible to answer. He could only provide Mabel with a frivolous response on that occasion, before making a swift exit.

'I often shout "God help me!" if I've messed up on something.' This caused them both to giggle hysterically.

Crispen decided that the café was becoming too raucous. The day was wearing on. He walked in the other direction away from Fleet Street and down the Strand towards Trafalgar Square.

Something had clicked into his thoughts when he remembered that he had been quite close to a trainee priest who had become an assistant at St. Martin-in-the-Fields church.

I wonder if he is still there, he thought. *There might be a chance of finding him there. Equally, he may have become an army chaplain, as many of them did.*

I will walk to St. Martin's. It will be good for me to see the place again anyhow, and the exercise will do me good.

Walking the length of the Strand proved to be a much longer walk than Crispen had anticipated. *I should have taken the bus,* he thought. When he arrived at St. Martin's his legs felt like lumps of lead. He was longing to sit down. He couldn't have managed another step.

Crispen found a seat at the back of the church. He removed his cap and placed it beside him on the pew, then put his head down, and said a silent prayer. A few moments later he was aware of someone coming towards him. He looked up to see an assistant verger.

'Can I help you at all, sir? I recognise your uniform. Are you just visiting us or are you on leave, waiting for a train?'

He sat up straight and moved his cap so that the verger could sit beside him. Crispen shook the verger's hand.

'Good afternoon, Verger. Actually, I am taking some accrued

leave, but I am here on a special mission. I am staying at the Union Jack Club for a few days before I can decide what to do next.'

Crispen explained that he had been at theological college with a friend who had, he thought, acquired a position at St. Martin-in-the-Fields church.

'I just wanted to ask if he was still here?'

'I am very sad to have to tell you,' the verger replied, 'that your young friend went to a military hospital in France and the first week he was there he was unfortunately caught up in a shell blast. It would have been very quick.'

'Oh, how dreadfully sad for his family. And such a great waste, of so many,'

'Yes, Sir. I agree,' said the verger. 'I'm afraid the conscientious objectors are having a tough time too. Some of them are attempting to organise a peace demonstration and they want to form a Peace Union. I have heard that they might be congregating in Trafalgar Square today. Just to warn you, Sir, in case you should become embroiled in the mass of angry people.'

'I must say that I sympathise with them in a way, but of course there will be different factions whose motivations are not simply anti-war.'

The verger asked Crispen about his own war experience.

'It was horrific. Sometimes I was forced to bury men where they had fallen. I saw men who avoided firing their rifles and took cover during periods of vicious conflict, only to be accused of desertion, or cowardice. Some were shot dead by their own officers.'

'How did you manage to return home?'

'I don't know whether I believe it was an act of providence, or something greater. I was with British and Australian land troops at Gallipoli when a massive allied rescue operation was begun. They had to get the men who were trapped on the beaches away as soon as they could. There were a number of rescue ships as well as warships hovering around the bay. Somehow I became separated from my unit. It was mayhem. I was pushed along with groups of soldiers that I didn't know. Eventually I was transferred to a large hospital ship along with the injured. That was the start of a most perilous time.'

'Do you wish me to continue?' Crispen asked.

'Please do, if you feel able.'

'It was a terrible shock. Most harrowing, of course, was my having to say prayers over so many dead soldiers, one after the other. Then there were the sea burials. I don't mind admitting that I felt inadequate, emotionally drained and as scared as everyone else did. It was a great relief to arrive in Malta. We were part of a great influx of injured soldiers to be taken to Mtarfa hospital.'

Crispen had to stop for breath. He hadn't meant to unburden himself like that. He realised that it was the first opportunity he'd had to speak of his ordeal, and here he was relating it all to a complete stranger.

'Verger, I most sincerely apologise for burdening you with my experience.'

'Nonsense, Chaplain. You are sharing your experience, not burdening me with it. Isn't that exactly what you would be doing with some of the soldiers we have here?'

Crispen looked up and around the church. He hadn't noticed the swelling numbers of uniformed soldiers who had taken quiet refuge in the church. He was told that there were many more soldiers below them, down in the crypt.

'We have opened the church all day and all through the night, now. Some of the soldiers are here waiting for transport to their troop trains. Some are here on home leave and find they have no home to go to. Some were badly injured and can't return to their regiments. We are trying to care for them in the first instance and then we try to find them a place to stay.'

Crispen was over-awed by the stories the verger had to tell. He was filled with admiration and would have offered his own services immediately, but he had to be practical, for the time being.

Crispen explained about Patient 355 and his own mission.

'I had it in mind to request a sabbatical year so that I could learn more about the treatment of psychological disorders. I have seen so many with shattered minds and shattered lives.'

'How far have you got with your application?' the verger asked.

'I haven't applied at all, yet. I need to check the requirements of my own commission first. I wonder if the powers that be would prefer me to return to the battlefields, or to remain here to help those soldiers and sailors who are in need here at home to re-build their lives.'

The verger looked at his pocket watch and asked Crispen if he would like to join him for tea in the crypt.

They took the steps down to the crypt below the church. The atmosphere was quite gloomy and rather cold now that the sun had disappeared.

'It's never actually warm down here,' the verger said.

'I can see that you are trying to make the soldiers more comfortable with the mattresses on the stone floor,' Crispen replied.

'I'm sure it's better than sleeping on the streets and December will not be far away now.'

Crispen chatted with a few of the soldiers. They seemed to appreciate the opportunity to talk about things other than war and destruction. They told him about their mothers, wives and children. Some told tales about their bullying sergeant-majors. Mostly they talked about what they would like to do when the 'ruddy' war was over. They moderated their language in front of Crispen and the verger.

The verger accompanied Crispen back upstairs and out towards the big outer doors of the church. He promised to return to St. Martin's to let them know what his future plans were.

'I have to return to St. Bart's Hospital tonight. I am trying to help a patient who was badly injured in Gallipoli. He has amnesia. We don't yet know his name, but I hope and pray that we may have a promising lead. Crispen asked the verger's advice about approaching the Old Highgate Vicarage.

'I used to know old Reverend Coombe. It must be over twenty or more years since he died,' the verger said.

Crispen said that he remembered it well.

'The present vicar at Highgate has a mansion. I believe the top floor of the mansion has been utilised as a children's convalescent home. Chaplain, I suggest you send a telegram. Keep it simple. I would give your full name and head it 'military matter'. You could then ask if it would be convenient to call on them at a time convenient to themselves. You could request a reply to the Union Jack Club.'

Crispen Honeybourn thanked the verger.

'I can't tell you how grateful I am for your advice. I feel quite heartened having visited St. Martin's, named for the soldier who became a bishop.'

'Come again, Chaplain. You will be most welcome at any time, night or day – that is, unless the zeppelins get us next time.'

It was too late to bother returning to the Union Jack Club before visiting St. Bart's again. He paid for another extravagant cab ride back to Smithfield Street. His legs deserved a rest. They ached so much after his very long walk, though the walk had been worthwhile. He had felt invigorated after his visit to St. Martin's and encouraged by his meeting with the verger. Now he had to think carefully about sharing or not sharing the events of his day with anyone at St. Bart's. That was, anyone except for Nurse Mabel Flowers.

Crispen was annoyed that he would have to make another long journey to collect the photographs. The shop assistant had quoted late afternoon. He thought he would telephone the shop in the morning, just on the off-chance that they might be ready sooner.

The carriage ride was a good idea. Crispen had pushed himself to the limits of his physical stamina that day. The nurses were pleased to see him and even Nurse Annie Vidler, now feeling more confident with Crispen dared ask if he had enjoyed 'gadding' around London by himself. He replied in the same vein of humour.

'I couldn't exactly say 'gadding' – more like crawling along. My legs are quite wobbly. Do you know I walked the whole length of the Strand?'

'You could have taken the omnibus, Chaplain.'

'I know, Nurse Annie. I was silly. I'm afraid I did cheat on the way back here and paid for a cab.'

'Well, now you must have something to eat,' insisted Nurse Mabel.

'What would you like? Some soup, a cheese sandwich, or both?'

'Soup would be wonderful. Thank you. That will warm me.'

'I will bring some on a tray. Would you like to sit in Sister's office? She gave us permission.'

'Thank you, Nurse Mabel. You are all so kind the way you look after me. Shall I go and visit our patient before I have the soup?'

The patient was sleeping, so Crispen decided to leave him. He would have the soup and then return to his club where he would have peace and quiet in order to compose the telegram.

Even if the Coombe family didn't know who the patient's friend Charlie was, it would certainly be a momentous visit for Crispen Honeybourn. He wondered, rather nervously what kind of reception he would receive. Of course, they might not even remember him. After all he couldn't have been much more than ten years of age when he was sent away to boarding school. He couldn't tell for himself whether his features had changed as he had grown up. He was still very slim and his straight hair could still be described as a mousey colour. He still wore spectacles which refused to stay put on the narrow bridge of his nose. He was still very short-sighted so he always had to have two pairs of spectacles. If he put one pair down to read without them, he needed to have a second pair in a safe place in case he couldn't locate the first pair.

He sat in Sister Mackintosh's room, writing a rough note for his intended telegram to Alice Coombe. Nurse Mabel returned with his soup.

'Here you are, Chaplain. I have brought some bread too. You can dip it in the soup if you wish.'

'Ahhh, lovely. It smells good, thank you. I'm afraid I have to ask for your help finding my spectacles. I took them off to write something. Now I can't find them.'

Nurse Mabel chuckled as she helped him locate the spectacles.

'Here they are, on the bookshelf. You are always losing them. Why don't you have them on a chain 'round your neck. Then they won't be lost!'

'Thank you, Nurse Mabel. You are the most practical person I know, and so thoughtful.'

'There you are. Put the soup spoon where you can see it,' she laughed, then returned to her ward duties.

Crispen Honeybourn was so tired that he almost nodded off to sleep in Sister Mackintosh's office. He managed to pull himself together and prepared to visit Patient 355 before he left the hospital.

'I thought I would take a last peep at him before I returned to the Union Jack Club.'

'He's been sleeping nearly all day,' Nurse Mabel said. She was looking rather serious as Crispen moved towards the patient's bedside.

'Has he been doing anything new?'

'We were concerned this morning. I didn't really want to tell you, but you would be sure to find out what the doctors did to him.'

'Tell me, Nurse Mabel, please.'

'One of the doctors sent two orderlies to transport the patient to the hydrotherapy pool. They said it was to get his legs moving now they have removed the plaster. We were all very shocked to see him when he was returned to us. He was very cold and shivering. We have been trying to keep him warm all day.'

Crispen Honeybourn was very concerned but tried hard not to show how cross he was feeling.

'I thought we had agreed with the doctors that water therapy was not the best idea just yet.'

'I'm afraid these doctors seem to do as they please. They think they are God!'

Nurse Mabel realised that was not the correct thing to say to Crispen.

'Oh, Chaplain, Crispen, I am so sorry for my clumsy words. I shouldn't have said that.'

'That's all right, Nurse Mabel. I agree with you. I suppose the doctors are nowhere to be seen again tonight?'

'No, I don't think so. The next rounds are at 10.00 a.m. for the junior doctors. The senior doctors arrive later.'

Chaplain Honeybourn, in his official capacity, took another look at the sleeping patient.

'Well, he seems to be fast asleep now. I won't wake him. He seems quite warm enough, Sister Mackintosh.'

Sister Mackintosh nodded, and then bade the Chaplain a good night, and safe journey back to the Union Jack Club. He spent another hour writing and re-writing the telegram to the Coombe family – well, at least, he addressed it to Alice Coombe.

He did precisely as the verger at St. Martin's had suggested. He included all the proper details of his name and rank and made a heading indicating – A Military Matter – then wrote a concise request:

Dear Miss Coombe,

I would very much appreciate your help regarding the above. May I call upon you soon, on a day and time of your convenience? I would be obliged if you could send a reply telegram, with the post boy, by return to myself addressed c/o The Union Jack Club, 91 Waterloo Road, London. I am, Yours faithfully, Crispen Honeybourn

It sounded polite without going into any elaborate details. That could wait until they were able to speak face-to-face together.

Having satisfied himself that the wording was correct and in order, he took a proper telegram form from the rack in his room. He wrote it out again in his neatest handwriting, checked it several times, and then took it to the clerk at the front desk.

'Will you be so kind as to make sure this telegram is sent at the earliest possible time? It is of the utmost importance.'

'I certainly will, sir. Are you expecting to receive a reply?'

'I hope so. I have requested a reply, by return.'

'If you are not here when the reply arrives, the telegram will be placed here in the rack, sir. The concierge will look after it until you are available.'

'Thank you, I am much obliged to you.'

'Goodnight, sir.'

'Goodnight to you.'

Crispen Honeybourn felt that, in spite of aching limbs, he had experienced a most satisfying day. He hoped that he would have a much better night's sleep. He knew that his brain would be working overtime. He was already worrying that if he went out to collect the photographs he might not be there to accept the telegram reply. He felt quite confident that he would receive a reply from Alice Coombe. What should he do? Should he stay in the club until the reply arrived, or risk going out for the photographs and hurrying straight back again?

He had another night of tossing and turning and eventually was fully awake by 6.00 a.m.

Crispen Honeybourn, you silly fool. What are you going to do for the next two hours before breakfast? he asked himself.

He took a leisurely bath and dressed very carefully in his pristine uniform. The Union Jack Club had arranged for the uniform to be professionally cleaned and pressed. Even the cap badge had been polished until it shone. He could see his face reflected in it.

He tried to read his newspapers, which had been delivered to his door, but he found it almost impossible to concentrate. Articles were mostly about the war, or the government. There were upsetting lists of war casualties, political rhetoric and a piece about the price of groceries. According to *The Times*, 'fish was plentiful this week'.

Crispen put the newspapers away and stood up to peer through the windows. The weather seemed bright enough, though he detected the first signs of frost appearing on the pavements.

Breakfast was being served. Although he wasn't particularly

hungry, he ordered boiled eggs and toast together with a pot of tea. That should keep him going until lunchtime, at least. He always lost his appetite whenever he was pre-occupied with something. He struggled with the eggs and decided that he would rather have had some fruit. Fruit was sometimes scarce, but somehow the Union Jack Club always seemed to find some. Logistically, he thought, it might have been a better idea to stay in a hotel on the Strand, but he knew that would have been very noisy, and besides, the Union Jack Club was a haven for soldiers and sailors. They looked after their clientele very well indeed.

Having decided that he would telephone the photographic shop early, Crispen stopped worrying about trivialities. The concierge rang the number for him.

'There you are, sir, they have answered.'

'Thank you.' He took the telephone from the concierge.

'Hello, hello, yes this is Chaplain Honeybourn at the Union Jack Club. I am calling to ask if my films are developed yet?'

'Yes, sir, they are just here on the counter, ready for you to collect.'

'Thank you very much. I will be there very shortly.'

Crispen Honeybourn lost no more time being annoyed that he had been told to collect in the late afternoon. *It wasn't worth worrying about,* he thought. *Just go and fetch them.*

'I will be back within the hour,' he told the concierge.

He didn't hesitate about hailing a cab this time. He asked the cabbie to wait for him and he was back in the Union Jack Club within the hour, clutching his packet of photographs.

Crispen didn't bother going to his room. He found a seat in the morning lounge and ordered some more tea. He couldn't wait to open the packet. He was like an excited child.

He was glad he had ordered three copies of everything. There they were. Clear photographs of the three of them. Nurse Mabel Flowers with the patient, Crispen with the patient, and a picture of the patient by himself, holding his walking stick. It was a pity the pictures were all in black and white. It would have been very nice to be able to see the lovely colours he had used on the stick.

It was just possible to see enough of the patient's face to gain an impression of the bandaged parts. Crispen was over-joyed. He was so glad that he had bought the camera. He may not have thought of it had the patient not drawn the sketch of Crispen.

Crispen Honeybourn, pleased with his purchase and the photographs, left the lounge to return to his room, when the concierge called him back.

'Chaplain Honeybourn, sir. The telegram boy is here. He has a telegram for you.' The boy waited.

'Is there a reply, sir?'

Crispen read the telegram.

We will be pleased to meet you at the Union Jack Club today at 1.00 p.m. Will that suit you?

Signed: Alice Coombe-Gardner and Alfred Richards.

'Yes! Yes! Yes, please!'

He gave the boy a shilling together with his reply.

The boy thanked him and ran off.

Crispen Honeybourn was consumed with nervous anticipation. On one hand, he was excited to be meeting Alice Coombe after so many years. On the other hand, he was more than a little anxious about her reason for preferring to make a journey into the city to meet him.

He didn't yet understand the relationship between Alice and Alfred Richards, but doubtless all would be revealed in due course. He would have to be patient. He instinctively knew there would be several interesting connexions to unravel.

Pacing up and down the corridors, stopping now and then to peer through the high windows, Crispen was hoping that the expected snow would not materialise that morning.

It would be awful if the weather prevented him from meeting Alice and Alfred. He was full of expectations.

He was trying to be positive. Crispen knew that he always spent far too long cogitating and worrying about speaking, especially with strangers. It was easy with church services and ceremonies. The words were usually set for him with pre-ordained prayers and sermons. He could rehearse and memorise words in those situations.

This time there were no set words, no precedent for him to rely on. He was completely responsible for his own words and his own approach to the unique situation before him.

By twelve noon, Crispen Honeybourn had settled his nerves and began to feel more relaxed. He decided to go for a very short walk in the fresh air and a little exercise. It would help to clear his head. He stopped to buy some violets from a small child who was helping her mother. They both looked very cold. He walked on in the direction of a tantalising smell of roast chestnuts. He bought two bags of chestnuts and walked back to give them to the flower sellers.

Crispen made his way back to the Union Jack Club. He was much calmer, but couldn't concentrate on reading. He tidied himself for the second time, or was it the third? He asked the concierge if there was a private place where he could meet his visitors, without being disturbed.

'What about the library, sir? I doubt whether anyone will be wanting to use that this morning. Would you like me to place a notice on the library door?'

'That would be an excellent idea, thank you very much.'

'You are most welcome, sir. Shall I just put a notice indicating PRIVATE MEETING?'

'That would be perfect, thank you again.'

Crispen had checked and checked again several times that the photographs were still safe in his pocket. Then he began to search for some careful words. He was aware that it was a delicate situation.

It was clear, as Crispen remembered reading through the navy records, that Charles was Alfred's son, and Alice was his aunt. He had previously only had a vague recollection of Frances. But now it was obvious to him that Frances was Alice's elder sister, and so she was Charles Richards' mother.

Crispen had huge hopes that the 'Charlie', whose name had been desperately screamed by Patient 355, was, in fact, Charles Richards. But what if it wasn't? He might be putting Alice and Alfred through even more agony. Either way, it was terribly sad for the Richards family. He just hoped and prayed that his instincts and all the careful research both he and Harry Abbott had done were correct.

He hovered nervously, pacing up and down the entrance lobby, waiting for a carriage to appear. He was certain that would be how his visitors would arrive. He was right. At exactly one o'clock a carriage stopped and the driver helped Alice safely on to the pavement. Alfred Richards paid the driver, then he steadied Alice as she took his arm.

Crispen knew instantly that it was Alice Coombe. Even after so many years he would have recognised her. She still had golden ringlets in her hair.

The concierge held the doors open for them.

Alice smiled as she offered Crispen her hand.

'It is so good of you to come here to meet me,' he said.

Alice introduced her brother-in-law.

'Crispen Honeybourn, Chaplain Honeybourn, please meet my brother-in-law, Mr Alfred Richards. He is married to my sister, Frances. Do you remember Frances?'

Crispen took Alfred's hand.

'I am pleased to meet you Chaplain,' Alfred said, and gave a small, polite bow.

'How do you do, Mr. Richards? Please come with me. We have a private place where we may talk.

'Crispen took his guests to the library. He offered them a warm drink, or maybe he could offer them a light lunch, later.

Alfred Richards replied for them both.

'No, thank you, Chaplain. We have a very busy schedule for

the next day or two. We have to get back to Highgate as soon as we can.'

'In which case I am doubly grateful that you have spared the time to come here.'

Alice couldn't wait to be heard.

'We decided that it would be better if we came here to meet you. Things are problematical at home. Your telegram was brief, but when you wrote that it was a military matter we assumed that it might concern my nephew, Charles.' Alice bit her lip to avoid the tears which would be certain to flow if she had to talk about Charles.

'Well, firstly, let me say how very sorry I was to discover your sad loss. I was quite astonished to discover your name and address when I was searching for another man's family. I will try to explain everything as fully as I remember the facts.'

Alice interrupted Crispen's flow of thoughts. She said that she remembered what a very serious little boy he had been when he came to live with her family. She explained the circumstances to Alfred.

'What an amazing quirk of fate that we should meet again like this, after all those years.'

'Yes, it is,' Crispen whispered, 'it's almost bittersweet. Serendipity, you might say.'

Crispen didn't dwell on his past life with the Coombe family. He promised to talk more about it later, if they wanted him to.

'Sadly, I have to refer to *HMS Goliath* and I sincerely regret having to make you re-live your terrible tragedy. I hope you will understand my mission. I am looking after a young man who survived the sinking of *Goliath*. He was very badly injured, and as a result of his head injuries and severe shock, he has just survived without a memory. We do not know who he is. Apart from the head injuries, he broke both his legs. He is now in St. Bart's Hospital and I continue to visit him.'

Alice and Alfred listened intently.

'I need to tell you that when the nurses tried to use the bath-trolley beside his bed, in order to wash him, he screamed when he saw his own face in the water. He must have been re-living the night the ship went down. He screamed for a man called Charlie. "Charlie, help me," he screamed.'

Alice put her hands up to her face.

'Please go on, Chaplain,' Alfred said.

Crispen swallowed hard. He explained that through a laborious process of steadily working through the crew lists and looking for anyone named Charles, or Charlie, they had managed to come up with a short list of possibilities.

'I guessed that for someone to use the familiar name of "Charlie", instead of Charles, they might have been friends as well as crew-mates.'

Crispen paused for a moment to wipe his brow.

'Do you wish me to continue?' he asked.

'Yes, please do, Chaplain.'

'My assistant clerk suggested we narrow the search further by finding Charlie or Charles crew members who were nearest in age to our patient. We were left with two names. When I looked for the home addresses of the two names and their next-of-kin, I saw your name, Alice. There were two entries, the other one I now know is yours, Mr. Richards. Of course, it still may be that we need to contact the family of the other Charles. It may still be a very long shot that you would recognise our patient as a friend of your Charles.'

All three of them sat very quietly with their own thoughts.

'Should we visit the patient?' Alfred asked.

'I can do better than that initially,' Crispen said.

He very carefully and slowly took the photographs from his pocket.

'Would you be prepared to look at these photographs? I took some, and a nurse at St. Bart's took the ones of myself with the patient.'

'We would like to see the pictures,' replied Alfred.

Crispen prepared them.

'It isn't a very pleasant sight.'

Alfred Richards took the photo first. His hands began to shake and all colour drained from his face. He was transfixed. Alice had to take the photograph from him.

'Alfred, it's Arthur Cole, Artie!'

Alice returned the picture to Crispen.

'We thought he had perished with Charles. They were best friends, since boyhood,' she cried.

'We were told, by the navy, that they were both missing, presumed drowned,' Alfred revealed.

Crispen explained that the St. Bart's' patient, now known to be Arthur, was making a steady recovery, physically. He was able to take a few steps, using crutches.

'I'm afraid he is still struggling mentally. He does not know who he is and the depression comes and goes. Sometimes I have managed to encourage him to draw.'

Crispen showed them the photograph again in which the patient is holding his walking stick.

'If you take a close look you will see the beautiful decoration he has drawn along the length of the stick.'

They hugged each other closely for several minutes.

Crispen sat beside them both, not speaking, but allowing them to assimilate the news.

'So, my hunch was correct?'

Alice confirmed that indeed it was correct.

Alfred Richards became calmer and wanted to fill in the wider family circumstances.

'The young man, Arthur, is the son of Alice's housekeeper, Lily Cole, and the grandson of my housekeeper, Violet Cole. We were led to believe that both brothers, Jim and Arthur, had both been lost at sea. Miraculously Jim had survived. He returned home just a week ago, in time to surprise everyone after Alice and Edward were married. Apparently, he and Charles had met up on leave, in Devonport, and they had exchanged diaries, in case they didn't make it home, Jim said.'

'So, you have Charles' diary, written shortly before they sailed in different ships.'

'Yes, that's about it.'

Alice was trying to comprehend the details they did have.

'Could the navy have made a mistake? If Jim Cole and Artie have survived, where is Charles?'

Crispen Honeybourn's heart ached for them all, but he felt he must be as truthful and helpful as he possibly could.

'Of course, we want to believe that Charles may have survived the explosions and sinking of *Goliath*, but the navy will have completed a full report by now based on what observers witnessed, and there will be some photographs somewhere. It will show how the ship was targeted. The survivors who can talk, will have done so by now. Arthur was very unfortunate in that he had massive head injuries and couldn't speak at all, or even remember what occurred. He is still living through the shadows, the nightmare of it all. But there will be others who have accounted for what happened that night. Arthur, by the way was not the only man to suffer a severe loss of memory. We may be able to find out much more, in time. You see, the rescue ships picked up anyone from the sea. They were not all placed in the same ships. Several other warships took survivors and they had to get away from Morto Bay as quickly as they could. I would just say, be patient and the truth will be established sooner or later.'

'What are we to do, Alfred?' Alice asked.

Both Alfred Richards and Alice Coombe, who was now Alice Gardner, were trying hard to understand whether they felt joyful to have found Arthur, or desperately, overwhelmingly sad for the loss of Charles. They felt both emotions at once.

Crispen sat quietly until he felt it appropriate to say anything more.

Alice and Alfred held each other's hands.

'I realise that this has been another shock for you to absorb,' said Crispen, 'but I am thankful that we have found Arthur's name and by such a turn of fate that I should find his family, and you.'

Alice managed a smile. Alfred asked what would happen to Arthur now.

'He may never recover completely, but I am praying that the more secure he feels and the more physically able he becomes, the more likely he is to remember things, even if they are just snippets at first. I have already seen small signs of him remembering day-to-day events.'

Alfred was trying hard to assimilate everything and decide upon the best course of action as to the family situation. Alice wanted to visit Arthur immediately.

'We must tell Lily and Mrs. Cole right away, and Jim, of course.'

'Now steady, Alice,' Alfred cautioned her, 'we have to do this slowly and carefully. We cannot swamp the poor patient before he is ready. It must be his family's decision first.'

Crispen asked if they would like him to leave them alone to talk by themselves.

'No, no, Chaplain. Please stay. We need your advice and very much welcome your support in this situation.'

Alfred understood Alice's desire to visit Arthur immediately. That was the kind of person she was.

Alice explained how her sister Frances had never recovered from the loss of Charles.

'She is convinced that he will be coming home to us. She is emotionally very fragile, which is why we came here to speak with you privately.'

'I understand completely. What wise and loving people you both are.'

Alfred continued the story.

'We had the most wonderful surprise when Jim, Arthur's elder brother, arrived after Alice and Edward's wedding. He brought Charles' diary with him. Apparently, they had met up on leave when they were in Devonport. They knew they would be posted to warships imminently.'

Alfred's voice now quivered with emotion, preventing him from saying any more. Alice continued the story.

'Charles had said, "take it to my aunt Alice if I don't get home. She will know what to do with it".' Alice said that Charles and Arthur had been best friends throughout their boyhood, and they had looked after him when Jim ran away to join the navy. That was after his Granda had died. He had been a master carpenter. He taught Arthur everything he knew about wood.

Alfred had regained his composure. He wanted to tell Crispen about the time Arthur made a very beautiful walking stick which he placed in his grandfather's coffin.

'It touched all our hearts to see how distressed the boy was, yet he could do this for his grandfather.'

Crispen had been listening intently and he was quite overcome with emotion, himself. It was all fitting into place.

'Arthur was a ship's carpenter, wasn't he?'

'Yes, he was,' said Alice. 'His grandfather would have been immensely proud of him.'

'Well, you might like to have this picture. Here he is sitting beside his hospital bed, holding the walking stick he made for me, after I had fallen into an acacia bush, in Malta.'

Alice and Alfred were astounded at the picture.

'Yes, as I recovered and he was steadily trying to walk, I gave him the stick to use. The most amazing thing for me was that he remembered the name of the wood. Acacia wood!'

Alice's mood lifted.

'That means that one day he will remember other things, and people too.'

'Well,' Crispen tried his best to give an honest opinion. 'I am no expert, but I would conjecture that given the right circumstances, and with the support of understanding carers, there may be further chinks of light in his memory. I must be a little bit guarded, since I am not a doctor, but I do hope and pray that he will recover sufficiently to live a useful and reasonably happy life amongst the people who love him.'

Alice, Alfred and Crispen together agreed that the next step should be to invite Jim Cole, Arthur's brother, to visit him first.

It would be only right and proper for Jim to decide when and where he shared the news about Arthur with their mother and grandmother, Violet.

Crispen Honeybourn wrote a short letter to Jim explaining the situation and inviting him to visit the hospital whenever he felt able to do so. Alice and Alfred would take the letter to Jim and break the news to him, privately.

Alice, preparing to leave, threw all decorum to the wind and hugged Crispen tight.

'I shall look upon you as my honorary brother forever.'

Alfred shook Crispen by the hand and thanked him.

'We will look after him, Chaplain Honeybourn, Crispen.'

Crispen Honeybourn was emotionally drained after his meeting with Alfred Richards and Alice Coombe. He was elated one minute and anxious the next. He had to keep reminding himself to calm down and deal with one thing at a time. Isn't that what he would advise his patients or congregation, when he had people to advise? Isn't that exactly what he had advised many soldiers at Gallipoli, not to forget the nurses? Many of them were very young, volunteers, who had left home for the first time.

'You give me strength, Crispen,' he recalled Mabel's words.

Nurse Mabel Flowers would be waiting anxiously for news of his mission to help Patient 355. He wouldn't bother eating a meal until he had returned to the hospital. He wasted no time in returning.

Sister Mackintosh was the first person he saw. He asked how Patient 355 was progressing.

'He is making steady progress with the walking. A few more wobbly steps each day. He has been very upset by being plunged into cold water. I want to ask the doctors not to persist with that, but it really isn't my place to say so.'

'You could tell them it is having an adverse effect.'

'Thank you, Crispen. I will try.'

'Then, so shall I have my say. I have some news, Sister.'

Crispen Honeybourn explained all that he had managed to discover on behalf of Patient 355.

'He now has a name, Sister. But we mustn't break it to him yet. His brother is being told today and I am awaiting a message from him. I have suggested that he come to visit first, before bringing his mother. They will both have such a shock seeing him for the first time. His mother had thought him drowned, presumed missing. I think the official term is "missing, presumed drowned".'

Sister Mackintosh was overwhelmed with the news.

'Crispen Honeybourn, you are magnificent. I can't believe all the time, trouble and effort you have been to on behalf of this young man. You are a wonderful person. You deserve a medal for this.'

'No, not a medal, Sister. These brave boys deserve the medals and I am sad to say there are many thousands of them. We can only do our best for them.'

Crispen asked about Mabel and the other nurses.

'I was hoping you wouldn't ask about Nurse Mabel, yet,' Sister Mackintosh winced.

'Why, what has happened here whilst I have been busy elsewhere? Is she ill?'

'No, Nurse Flowers is perfectly well. It is Mary Wilson. You remember they are boarding at the nurses' home.'

'Yes, I do remember. Nurse Wilson had a nasty ordeal aboard the hospital ship.'

'That's correct. Well, the miscreant is now locked up in jail, but the publicity surrounding the case has frightened her and she has absconded. Nurse Flowers and Nurse Bell are combing the streets, looking for her.'

'Has she gone to her family?'

'We don't know yet, Crispen.'

'Well, I am sorry to hear about that. I'm sure she will re-appear when she feels brave enough.'

Crispen, Chaplain Honeybourn, resumed his official position as Hospital Chaplain, talking with patients as he moved through the wards. Some were long-term casualties from the war and some were newer patients caught up in the zeppelin bombings around

London. Until he met some of the newer patients, mostly from the East End, he had almost forgotten that London was still a target for the German zeppelins.

He found Patient 355. He was sitting up in his chair. He looked rather paler than Crispen remembered him from a few days ago.

His patient did manage a smile for Crispen.

'You remember me, then?'

The patient nodded, then took hold of his stick.

'Walk, walk,' he stumbled over the words, but they were quite clear. He wanted to walk.

'Come on then, old chap. Shall we do the whole ward?'

The patient eased himself from the chair. Crispen took his arm. Then, little by little, one slow step after another they walked the length of the ward without stopping.

'Well done!' Crispen said.

'Good, walk,' the patient replied.

The walk back to the patient's chair was more of a struggle, but the look of pleasure on the man's face cheered Crispen.

Crispen wondered whether he could, or should, reveal whatever he had discovered about his family. He gave it a huge amount of thought that night. *If I say nothing at all,* thought Crispen, *and then the patient is suddenly faced with his family, he could be very shocked, but he may equally be overjoyed.* Crispen had no real way of knowing which way would be wisest.

When Crispen Honeybourn returned to his Union Jack Club that evening, the concierge handed him another telegram, from Alfred Richards. He had written on behalf of Jim Cole.

Dear Chaplain Honeybourn. We have spoken with Jim Cole. He is overjoyed. I would like to bring him to St. Bart's myself. We will arrive around noon. I trust this will be in order. I remain, Yours truly, Alfred Richards. No need to reply.

Crispen breathed a sigh of relief. He didn't have to wrestle with the problem of how or when to reveal the patient's identity. They would do it together, though he thought it best to prepare the patient for the fact that he was going to be receiving a visitor.

Crispen hardly slept that night and was up very early the next morning. He made his way to the hospital before the doctors were proposing another cold bath for the patient.

'I am sorry, Sister. The doctors will have to delay the therapeutic bath this morning. We have something much more important to do.'

He grinned, and Sister Mackintosh was very curious.

'What are you up to now, Chaplain?'

'Wait and see, Sister. Wait and see.'

Crispen Honeybourn, Chaplain Honeybourn that morning, had arrived earlier than usual. He had several military patients to visit. He felt that he had been neglecting them since worrying about Patient 355. The other patients were very understanding and often asked how the patient was progressing.

'Sister Mackintosh tells me that they might remove most of his face bandages this morning,' he told one of his patients.

'That'll be great for him, won't it, Chaplain?'

'Yes, I'm sure it will. I can't imagine how it feels to be unable to wash your face properly, or to shave.'

'Good excuse to grow a beard then, Chaplain?'

The nurses have been very good helping him to shave whatever parts of his face they could reach.'

'What did I hear about the nurses?' a voice behind him said playfully. It was Nurse Mabel Flowers, just coming on duty.

'Good morning, Nurse Mabel. I am so pleased to see you this morning. I missed you yesterday. Did you find Nurse Wilson?'

'No, I'm afraid we didn't. We will continue the search later. We have alerted the police, but they are so busy just now I doubt they will bother looking for her, but at least they have a good description of her.'

'Well, let's hope she doesn't come to any harm,' sympathised Crispen.

'Mabel, sorry, Nurse Mabel, I have some very good news for a change.'

'Do tell, Chaplain. We could do with some good news.'

'It's about our Patient 355.'

'Have you found something?' she asked.

'Yes! We have found his name, his family, and his brother will be coming here just before lunchtime, to see him. They were told that he was missing, presumed drowned.'

'How amazing, Chaplain. I am so thrilled for him. You have been amazing too, following every possible lead. You never gave up hoping, and praying too, I guess?'

'Well, it hasn't all been down to me. It has been team work all round.'

'Can you tell me his name, Chaplain?'

'I will tell you everything, once his family have seen him.'

'I understand, Chaplain. I will be patient.'

Chaplain Honeybourn had managed to find a new set of pyjamas and a smart hospital-type dressing gown for the patient. The nurses had carefully washed the patient, taking extra special care around the areas of his face which were now uncovered. He was badly scarred, but Crispen Honeybourn had warned Alfred to alert Jim Cole what to expect when he first saw his brother.

'Now, you are looking quite smart this morning,' he greeted his patient.

'Face bad,' the patient struggled to speak as he pointed to his face.

'But it is looking much better. It will improve in time.'

The patient nodded.

'Do you know why we have had you dressed in new clothes and made you especially smart today?'

The patient shook his head and looked directly into Crispen's eyes.

'Do you remember that I had a few days off, looking for your family?'

The patient looked anxious and began to rock back and forth on his chair.

Crispen took hold of his hands.

'Now, try to sit still and listen to me. Be calm. There is nothing for you to be anxious about. I have found your family. Your brother is coming to see you today, in about an hour's time. We will take you to Sister Mackintosh's office so that you can meet in private.'

Chaplain Crispen Honeybourn was relieved that he had managed to find the words. He had spoken very gently and slowly so that the patient could take it all in. The Chaplain breathed a sigh of relief.

'You come,' the patient stuttered. 'You there?'

'I will be with you if that is what you wish, Arthur. Your name is Arthur.'

'Arthur,' he repeated, slowly.

Nurse Mabel Flowers, watching the Chaplain and his patient from a distance, knew that the Chaplain had told the man his name.

Nurse Mabel felt very emotional watching the scene unfold. She knew that Crispen would have a large lump of emotion in his throat too. She went to their rescue.

'Would you like me to wheel Arthur to Sister's office?'

'Thank you, Nurse Mabel. We are both going to await the patient's visitor.'

Shortly before noon, just as Alfred Richards had indicated in his telegram, he had arrived at the ward door, accompanied by Arthur's brother, Jim Cole.

'Chaplain Honeybourn, good morning. May I introduce you to Jim Cole, your patient's brother?'

'Good morning to both of you. I can't tell you how very pleased I am to meet you. We have prepared Sister's office for you. I will be guided by you now. How would you like to proceed with meeting Arthur? I should warn you that he has a lot of facial scarring and he may not recognise you. He may become agitated. If you wish me to be in the room with him, I will do so. If you prefer to be completely private, then please say so.'

Jim Cole asked directly whether the Chaplain had asked the patient what he would like to happen.

'Yes, he asked me to be there.'

'Then that is what we will do,' said Jim.

Chaplain Honeybourn opened the door to the office and sat beside the patient. Jim and Alfred Richards followed.

'Arthur, this is your brother, Jim.'

'Jim, this is your brother, Arthur.'

Jim immediately hugged his brother so tight, it seemed as though he would never let him go. Arthur did the same.

Jim then sat down beside his brother. Chaplain Honeybourn and Alfred Richards moved out of their way. They allowed Jim to speak with his brother, without interrupting their conversation. In fact, the conversation was mostly one-sided. Jim quickly realised that his brother had difficulty remembering and then forming words clearly. He was trying to make an effort to reply to questions. It was obvious that Arthur's ability to recall events and people was severely limited. Arthur seemed happy for that moment just to be with Jim. He was smiling and holding on to Jim's arm. He didn't want to let go.

'How do you feel, Artie?'

'Artie? Artie? Artie?' his brother replied.

He seemed very confused and Crispen anticipated some sort of agitation might follow. He had to join in the conversation.

'We told him that his name was Arthur,' Crispen said. 'We weren't aware at that time, that he had a more familiar name amongst his family.'

Jim was bright enough to understand the situation. He had already encountered similar cases to Arthur's, and many of them were more severe.

'It is as though we have to take Arthur back to the very beginning. In a way, he is starting again, just like a child.'

Crispen explained that words which were given to Arthur the previous week were beginning to take root in his memory.

'I can see some signs of recognition.'

Jim was distressed to see his brother in such a state, but he was grateful that he was alive and had people caring for him. He tried to speak with Arthur again.

'How are you today, Arthur?'

Arthur took a few moments to find the words. He kept hold of Jim's arm.

'Hap-py,' he struggled to string the syllables together.

'Then I am happy too.'

Jim turned to Crispen.

'Should I tell him about our mother and grandmother, yet?'

'I think it is probably a good idea, but I suggest you try to keep the words very simple, for now. He can soon begin to feel over-loaded with information and then he is liable to become very frustrated.'

Jim waited until he was sure that he had proper eye contact with Arthur.

'Are you listening to me, Arthur?'

'Ye-s-s,' Arthur drawled.

'Our mother, Lily and our grandmother, Violet, are waiting to look after you, when you are ready to leave hospital.'

'Lily, Li-ly, flower?'

'Yes, Lily is the name of a flower.'

'Vi-o-let, flower?'

Jim looked once more to Crispen for his advice.

'He is doing very well, Jim. Do not be alarmed. It will take time, but he is improving all the time.'

Jim was alarmed enough to question the wisdom of bringing their mother and grandmother to the hospital. Alfred Richards, witnessing these very personal moments, had been carefully considering ways in which he could offer help to Charles' closest boyhood friend. Charles would have wanted him to do that.

Alfred Richards and Crispen Honeybourn left the two brothers alone for a few minutes. They stepped out of the office and Alfred came straight to the points he wished to raise.

'Chaplain, may I call you Crispen?'

'Of course you may.'

'Crispen, I would very much like you to see how I have adapted my house in Kensington. I acquired a very large mansion house after my father's death. To be honest I thought it most obscene to have all that space to live in. You will be amazed to see an art gallery and a workshop for artists and craftspeople. Arthur's grandfather, Jim, helped me with all the wood for the furniture, the picture frames and so much more. In addition to all of that, I have created a social help centre where soldiers and sailors who are homeless can stay for a while. I can help them learn a trade and they can receive food and health care until they can stand on their own two feet. I would like Arthur to come and see the place when he is well enough to do so.'

Crispen was taken aback.

'Forgive me. I had no idea of your house, or the gallery and workshop. What an amazing idea, and such generosity on your part. I would very much like to visit, with Arthur. It could be the very haven that he needs just now.'

'I am offering a home,' said Alfred. 'We will take care of him. His grandmother is my housekeeper and mostly spends her time caring for my wife, Frances, but she is an amazing lady. She has volunteered most generously to help in our centre kitchens.'

'What about Arthur's mother, Lily?'

'Lily now keeps house for my sister-in-law, Alice, and her new husband, Edward Gardner.'

'Is Lily a live-in servant?'

'No, she maintains a small house in Kentish Town, which was their family home, but things there would not be suitable for Arthur right now.'

'How would you feel, Alfred, if I brought Arthur to visit your house one day soon? Both Jim and I feel it would be too shocking for his mother and grandmother to visit the hospital. Jim could prepare them and we could bring Arthur there to meet them all together.'

'That sounds to me like a very sensible idea, Crispen. I hope it wouldn't be too overwhelming for Arthur, but let's face facts. He will have to deal with the situation very soon. The hospital will not keep him forever.'

185

'I will speak with the doctors, Alfred. His facial injuries are healing quite well, despite scarring, which may be permanent. His bones appear to have mended, though they were badly set, in a hurry, in Malta. We are told that he will always walk with a limp. The only area I am not very happy with is the very laissez-faire attitude some of the doctors show over the use of psychotherapy.'

Alfred grimaced.

'Oh, that! I can tell you I have had a very trying time with my wife, Frances. The doctors have grown quite impatient with her. She is drugged all the time to keep her quiet.'

'Grief can be all-consuming, Alfred. Tablets aren't really the whole answer. She has to be helped to come to terms with her grief and loss. It could be a long process, as it surely will be with Arthur. I'm afraid that one of the difficulties for the medical people is that, although there are wonderful doctors making great advances in restorative work on physical injuries and rehabilitation, the psychiatric services are less developed and rather patchy.'

The doctors at St. Bart's were fully in favour of Chaplain Honeybourn taking Arthur Cole to visit the Kensington centre. They agreed that there was little more they could offer him, other than keeping bandages changed and his flesh cleaned. If people were able to help him walk each day, they thought his muscles would soon become stronger. They were happy to discharge him from being a fulltime patient. Suggestions were offered regarding what the doctors described as therapeutic cold baths. Crispen assured the doctors that Arthur would receive all the therapies he needed, but in a private capacity. Alfred Richards would see to that.

Alfred Richards took it upon himself, as he had promised, to visit Arthur every day for the next week, to assist with his walking. At first they walked the length of the ward, up and down. Then, as Arthur became more confident, they walked the long hospital corridors. Eventually they had a short walk outside to the gardens nearby.

Crispen Honeybourn caught up with them both on the last day.

'Good morning, Arthur. How are you doing today?'

186

'Good mor-ning, chap-chap-lain. G-ood.'

'Good morning, Crispen. Arthur is trying so hard. He is much less tired than he was last week.'

'Are you set for tomorrow's visit then, Arthur?'

Arthur responded with a huge grin and nodded enthusiastically.

'Who will be taking you to Kensington? Do you remember?'

Arthur had to concentrate hard.

'Jim, one.' He held up one finger, as he had been told, 'Chaplain, two.' He held up two fingers. 'Mis-ter Rich-ards, three.' He held up the three fingers.

'Well done, Arthur,' Crispen encouraged him.

'And who is meeting us there?'

Arthur couldn't remember. He shook his head, crossly.

'Perhaps we have over-taxed him, Alfred? Never mind. One thing at a time. He is setting the pace for us, isn't he?'

Crispen agreed.

Arthur was awake earlier than usual the next morning. It was bright and sunny, if a little chilly. Nurse Mabel Flowers and Nurse Betty Bell came early too. They helped him to dress. He refused breakfast scones, but managed to drink his tea without spilling it on the smart clothes that Crispen had found for him.

'I do hope it all goes well for him, and for you too, Crispen,' Mabel whispered in Crispen's ear.

'So do I, Nurse Mabel. I will be here tomorrow to tell you all about it. I have something else to ask you, but it will keep until then.'

The nurses walked Arthur and his three companions down to Alfred Richards' waiting carriage. The nurses stood on the steps of the hospital to wave them goodbye.

Arthur had never been for a ride in such a grand carriage, but seeing the black horse triggered something in his brain. He fidgeted constantly with his walking stick and ran his fingers up and down the colourful pictures he had drawn. He kept his eyes on the black horse, ignoring all the other road traffic and the people going about their normal daily business.

187

The carriage pulled up outside Alfred Richards' mansion. Alfred spoke to the driver before helping Arthur down to the pavement. Then Alfred took Arthur by his right arm and Crispen took his left arm. Jim Cole walked in front of the threesome, almost like a procession.

Jim Cole was bursting with pride and excitement to be taking his brother to meet their mother, Lily, and his grandmother, Violet.

They had been prepared about what to expect of Arthur the first time of meeting him again. They too were filled with nervous anticipation.

Jim cautiously opened the big outer door and walked in first, ahead of Arthur and his companions. Lily was overcome when she saw poor Arthur. His grandmother, Violet, was silently tearful. She took Lily's hand.

'Come on, girl. Here is your son. Welcome him home.'

Crispen and Alfred let go of Arthur.

Lily ran towards him and took him by the hand. His grandmother took his other hand. There were no big speeches or frantic hugs and screams. There was no talking either for a while.

Jim Cole led them to the Gallery. They sat down on the benches which Arthur and Jim's grandfather had made. Arthur ran his fingers over the wood, remembering.

'Granda Jim,' he said suddenly.

It was then that the tears and the emotional hugs came in great profusion.

Crispen Honeybourn and Alfred Richards crept out of the Gallery and left them alone, in private.

'Thank you, Crispen, for everything. The words simply are just not enough for what you have done.' Crispen was choked with emotion too. He found it difficult to describe exactly how he felt. He promised to return the next day.

'I will go now and leave you in peace,' he said seriously. 'There is something very important I must do.'

Crispen Honeybourn had witnessed the most wonderful happening that day. He had felt privileged to share the reunion with

Arthur and his family. They in their turn would be forever grateful to Chaplain Crispen Honeybourn. Alfred Richards acknowledged that Crispen had acted far beyond the realms of duty.

Crispen couldn't contain himself any longer. He hurried back to St. Bart's as quickly as he could. He found Nurse Mabel Flowers relaxing in the gardens near to the hospital.

'Crispen, how was it? We didn't expect you back again today.'

'Mabel, it was astonishing and wonderful. I had to come back to share it with you.'

'Slow down, Crispen. Tell me slowly.'

He took a deep breath.

He took Mabel by the hands.

'I want you to tell me something first, Mabel. Dear, lovely, kind and sensitive, wise and loving Mabel.

'Will you marry me?'

'Crispen! Are you sure?'

'I've never been more sure of anything in my life, Mabel.'

'When?' she asked excitedly.

'Christmas, let's do it at Christmas?'

'Mabel Flowers, will you marry me at Christmas?'

Crispen knelt down in front of her and Mabel giggled.

'Who do I need to ask?'

'I'm over twenty-one now, Crispen. I can decide for myself.'

'Well, what is your answer?' he pleaded.

'Yes, Crispen Honeybourn. I would love to marry you.'

'Shall we try for St. Martin-in-the-Fields?'

'Yes, let's try for that,' Mabel said, planting a gentle kiss on his forehead.